AF485962

The Mystery of the Element Stones

AUTHOR NAME:

Shreya Sudesh Shinde

Copyright © 2012

Author Name: Shreya Sudesh Shinde

All rights reserved.

ISBN: 9798813312144

DEDICATION

I dedicate this book to my readers.

CONTENTS

The Mystery of the Element Stones

ACKNOWLEDGMENTS

This book is possible only because my parents have motivated me to always take up new challenges and supported me in every aspect of life.

I take this opportunity to thank my parents, mentors, teachers, family and friends. I would also like to thank Colorscapes, Color Art, Paint by Number, Tap Color Pro and Coloring Book for the aesthetic pictures.

Introduction

This Story is set in various dimensions and is the continuation of 'The Mystery of the Questionable Past'.

1 What are Elemental Stones?

It was 3 am in the unknown… Layla, Axel, Priscilla and Max reached the unknown, and flew swiftly across the navy-blue sky…

They soon reached the Dummy Millennium Castle and entered the corridor. They went straight to the living room and settled down.

Axel looked out the window and concluded, "Looks like there's going to be a storm…"

"Storm? I thought time was different in all dimensions, not the weather…", stated Layla, walking towards the window.

"Everything is different in all dimensions, including the weather… Sometimes, a year in one dimension can be only a day in another dimension…", replied Max, stretching.

"Yeah… But this storm looks unusual…", stated Axel, studying the clouds.

"What do you mean?", questioned Priscilla,

standing up.

"Look at the pattern of the clouds. In this dimension, they usually form a moon like structure. But now… It's something else…", replied Axel, pointing at the shape of the clouds.

"Shape of the clouds?", questioned Layla.

"Each dimension has a specific aura. The clouds always form a specific shape. In the human world, clouds are of various shapes since all humans have different unique qualities.

This dimension, for a particular reason, always has moon-shaped clouds, during storms and all other times.", replied Axel.

Max sensed something and also walked over to the window. He quickly analyzed the cloud shape and concluded, "Looks like a… staff…"

"Staff?", questioned Priscilla, confused.

"Yeah, you know the thing which some royals carry, it looks kind of like a wand.", replied Max, casually.

Axel thought about this and looked at the cloud.

After Max mentioned the staff, Axel could now identify the shape! He then looked at the top of the staff. Then he realized something.

"Hey, Max! Does that thing on top of the staff, look like a crystal?", questioned Axel, unsure.

Max looked at the cloud and assured Axel that it was a crystal.

"Huh? What do you guys think it symbolizes?", asked Axel, looking at the others.

Suddenly, the ground shook! The floor trembled and the four rushed out of the Castle without wasting a second.

The four then looked at the forest that surrounded the castle.

That's when Axel spotted something.

"Look! Reindeers!", stated Axel, pointing at the two majestic creatures.

"Guys… I may not know what that staff-shaped cloud symbolizes… But I think it's associated with that!", exclaimed Layla.

The three turned their gaze to where Layla pointed. They saw thunder growling! The lightning was hitting the trees and making them collapse!

Layla didn't waste a second and sped towards the reindeers at the speed of light.

She caught hold of the reindeers and teleported them to where the others were.

The reindeers directed their direction to where they were, and noticed that a tree would've collapsed on them if Layla hadn't teleported them!

The reindeers turned to Layla and hugged her. Layla smiled and hugged them back. The reindeers then bowed and disappeared into the forest.

"That was very nice of you Layla. Luckily, you noticed that the tree would collapse, otherwise the reindeers would've been terribly hurt.", stated Priscilla, smiling.

Max and Axel agreed with Priscilla and Layla smiled and thanked them.

"Guys, we need to find the source to that lightning and also find out if the change in the shape of the clouds is connected to the lightning.", said Axel. The others agreed and the four teleported to the library. They searched vigorously through the history section for quite a while.

After a few minutes, Max stated, "I found something! It's on the Element Stones!"

"Maybe that book could help us in some way?", questioned Priscilla.

"Maybe… Let's check it out!", exclaimed Layla, heading over to the table.

They reached the table and placed the book on the table. The book let out dust as it landed on the table with a thump! sound.

"Looks like no…one's read this book for a long time…", stated Priscilla, coughing.

"Yeah…", agreed Max, looking at the contents page.

While Max was reading the contents, the book suddenly flipped its pages! It then stopped at a blank page…

"Probably the wind…", said Axel, turning the pages.
But the book refused to show them any other page and flipped back to the blank page.

"Wow… The book really wants us to look at this page…", stated Layla, looking at the blank page, trying to spot any text.

After a while, the four were trifle-bewildered. There was neither any text on the page nor would the book allow them to go to any other page.

Priscilla then placed her palm on the book and studied the page.

Priscilla then concluded, "It's not having any indents either…"

Max thought about this for a while and looked around the table. He then caught hold of a glass of water and looked around the page with it, to see if there was some kind of ink that could only be seen with water.

However, this was a mare's nest…

Axel then placed his palm on the page and… light a fire on it!

"Axel! The book's going to burn!", exclaimed Max, about to light out the fire with the water he had previously grabbed.

Axel held onto Max's hand and looked at the others with a convincing smile.

Max decided to trust Axel, and retreated his hand from pouring the water.

Soon, the fire was absorbed by the page and some text was visible. The text was formed by the fire, and was part of the burnt part of the page.

"There are many elements present in this world. However, the most powerful ones, are in the possession of its guardians…

There are 9 powerful elements… However, we feel that it is not safe to mention them or their location… But what we can mention, is that some creature is out there, who wants these elements in their possession.

All creatures have an element; however, the most powerful ones are present in the form of stones…

The Mystery of the Element Stones

These stones when used together, can be used to help many creatures, but in the wrong hands, it could result in the taking away of all other element powers from other creatures.", narrated Axel.
"Who wrote this?", questioned Layla, looking at the others.

"Someone who was aware of the future…", answered Max.

"Axel… How'd you know that putting the page on fire would reveal the text?", questioned Layla, confused.

"I didn't know actually. It was just a gut.", replied Axel, honestly.

That's when the ground trembled again! The four looked out the window and saw the lightning strike something around the Dummy Millennium Castle.

"Oh No!", exclaimed Axel, teleporting outside the Castle.

The others sensed danger and teleported beside Axel. They noticed Axel using his powers to strengthen the shield around the castle.

The three, without thinking, started to help Axel strengthen the shield.

After a while, they managed to strengthen the shield! The four teleported to the library and looked at the book.

The book then flipped its pages to another page, with a symbol.

Layla placed her finger on the text and narrated, "Beware of this staff…"

She then looked at the staff given below the text. Her eyes then grew small with fear and she turned the book to the others.

When the others saw the staff, a shiver ran down their spines.

"Isn't that the staff that the clouds have formed?", questioned Priscilla.

Axel nodded slowly, his eyes trembling with fear.

"What do we do now? I mean, the book looks like it's given us all the info it could.", questioned Max, flipping the pages.

That's when another strike of lightning hit the shield around the castle.

"For now, we need to take a few essentials from here and leave! The shield won't be able to hold for long. That lightning is unusually strong.", stated Axel, looking outside the window.

The others nodded and the four split up. Axel went to Gardeniam and collected about 8 but very specific plants.

Layla headed to the 'lab' of the library and grabbed the Austin's nectar, a piece of paper, a few books on various powerful spells and the Marsium extract.

Max headed to the history section of the library and collected all the books he could find related to the element stones and the staff, and found about 6 books.

Priscilla rushed outside the castle and found chariot in the front lawn, petrified by the lightning. She calmed chariot down about the *lightning and told him that they were about to teleport to another dimension, so chariot would have to teleport to another dimension and keep himself safe.*

Chariot listened to Priscilla intently and agreed to do so.

The four then reunited at the library table and confirmed if they collected everything. That's when Axel recalled that he had forgotten a few other things.

He looked out of the window and instructed, "You guys wait for me in the front lawn, I need to get a few things."

"I'll go with you!", volunteered Layla.

Axel nodded and the four spilt up again, with Max and Priscilla heading out to the front lawn, and Axel and Layla heading to the second floor of the castle.

Axel instructed, "Go and get Nicole! I'll the the violin!"

That's when Layla realized why Axel was in such a rush back at the library! He wanted to collect the violin and Nicole. She obeyed Axel and entered the room where Nicole was.

Nicole spotted Layla and smiled. She then asked, "Hi Layla! Is there a storm outside? I have been hearing a lot of lightning and-"

Before Nicole could say anything else, she was being carried by Layla outside the room in a rush!

"Ok… What's going on?", questioned Nicole, skeptical.

"I'll explain later…", answered Layla, rapidly.

She met up with Axel in the connecting gallery and the two teleported outside, where Priscilla and Max had been waiting for them.

"Finally! You guys are here! We need to get out of here! And Fast!", exclaimed Max, flying around in his mythical form, panicking.

"Which dimension should we go to though?", questioned Priscilla.

"I know one…", answered Axel, snapping his fingers and teleporting themselves to an unknown dimension.

2 A Volcanic Dimension

The four teleported to another dimension. When they landed on the grass, they looked around.

Suddenly, Layla noticed something. She questioned, a shiver running down her spine, "Why is there a volcano here?"

"Oh! I forgot to mention one thing. This dimension is Volmania. The dimension of fire."

"The fire dimension?", questioned Max.

"Yeah, I thought that we could try and find those element stones and try and find the creature who it will bond with. That way, we'll be able to figure out what exactly is the history of these element stones.", replied Axel.

"Oh, great idea!", exclaimed Layla, smiling.

"Well...", said Priscilla.

"Where in this dimension will we find a tiny stone!?", questioned Priscilla, frustrated and looking at the endless looking path.

That's when the ground trembled. The four turned their gaze to the volcano and saw that sparks of fire were flying off from the top of the volcano.

"That's the active volcano of this dimension. One of the things this dimension is popular for.", stated Axel.

"One of the things!?", questioned Max, shocked.

"Yeah...", replied Axel, honestly, smiling.

"Hopefully, it will be easy to find that stone...", wished Layla, thinking of lava coming out of the volcano.

"So, what creatures live here?", questioned Max.

"Umm… Dra…Dragons…" replied Axel, stuttering.

"Dragons?", questioned Priscilla, confused. "Aren't they native to Dragonsville at the Enchanted Forest?"

"No, actually. They are native to Volmania. Majority of the dragons live here, including the most powerful ones…", replied Axel.

"How do you know all this?", asked Layla.

"Like I told you guys before, I have known magic for a very long time…", replied Axel, looking at the pathways.

"Odd…", thought Layla to herself. "He told me about how he encountered the Dummy Millennium Castle, but he never told me about when he started to study magic…"

"Two paths… We might need to spilt up…", stated Max.

"You're right. Layla and I can go down this path leading to the forest.", said Axel, looking at the left.

"That's means we have to go to the...", questioned Max, trembling with fear.

"Yes, Max. The volcano. Don't worry! It's just a volcano that hasn't erupted.", reassured Priscilla.

"Yet! It might erupt anytime...", said Max, scared.

Little did the others know, was that Max didn't like being near volcanoes.

Priscilla walked over to Layla and Axel and stated, "I'll look after Max. You guys need to head to that forest."

That's when Layla realized something and stated, "It's already sunset!"

"Oh, yeah! We might need to get a rain check about going down these two paths...", stated Axel.

"Phew! No Volcano!", exclaimed Max, relieved.

The others looked at Max, giving him a look.

"I mean… uh…", stuttered Max, unsure about what to say.

"I think we should go down the paths.", interrupted Priscilla, firmly.

"It's going to be dark soon. Are you sure?", questioned Layla.

"Yes. If we delay this till tomorrow, who knows what might happen because of the creature who resembles that 'staff'.", replied Priscilla, sure about her decision.

"Ok. When it gets dark, we'll just have to find a safe place to rest for the night. Sounds good?", stated Axel.

"Aye, Aye Captain!", exclaimed Layla and Priscilla, in unison.

"Uh-huh…", said Max, in a low voice, looking at the volcano.

"Adios Amigoes!", said Layla and Axel, in unison, walking towards the forest, waving.

Priscilla turned to Max and said, "Don't worry Max... It's just a volcano... Even if it does erupt, I could use my powers to protect us!", reassured Priscilla, smiling.

Max gulped hard and nodded. The two then walked down the path that led to the volcano.

Layla and Axel on the other hand had entered the forest and searched every single place for the fire stone. But they couldn't find it.

After walking 4 km into the forest, Axel looked up and stated, "Looks like it took us an hour or something to go 4 km deep into this forest while searching for an extremely small fire stone..."

"Yeah... So, where should we rest for the night? This forest looks like it only consists of trees...", questioned Layla, looking at the tall trees.

"Maybe we can sleep in the trees as little birds. That way, not many creatures would notice us, and we can sleep without any fear!", exclaimed Axel.

"Shh!!", shushed Layla, looking around.

"Sorry...", whispered Axel.

The two shapeshifted into two birds that could barely be seen in the faint light provided by the Moon.

The Mystery of the Element Stones

The night was very calm. Grasshoppers hopped their way back home, the stars twinkled in the midnight blue sky like small pieces of diamonds, and the Moon sparkled majestically in the sky, borrowing the golden light from the Sun, and converting it into pearl white light...

The wind whistled a tranquil tune, one that flows through the air like a wave and travels an endless journey through many universes...

~

Priscilla and Max started their journey by entering the grassland on the opposite side. The two walked down the path, with Priscilla breathing in the fresh air which swirled around the dimension and Max frightened.

"Isn't it just so wonderful here? The wind is swirling almost as if understands us and is playing!", exclaimed Priscilla, joyfully hopping around.

Max looked around for a while and noticed the spectacular beauty of Volmania. He also realized that Priscilla was right.

The wind did feel like it was playing by swirling

around the Volmania.

"Yeah, the wind does calm things down a bit…", stated Max, taking in a deep breath.

"We should start searching this place now, we need to find that fire stone.", remarked Priscilla, beginning to search.

Max nodded and the two searched for a very long time…

After a few hours passed by and the night conquered the sky and filled the sky with the twinkling stars and the majestic Moon.

"Phew! Its night already…", stated Max, looking up.

"Mhmm… Let's call it a day.", added Priscilla, looking around.

She then spotted a cave!

"Let's go there", said Priscilla, pointing at the cave.

"Sure. Only if you promise to use your powers and light up that dark cave…", stated Max, firmly.

The Mystery of the Element Stones

Priscilla chuckled and agreed to do so.

The two walked down the path that led to the cave and entered it.

Priscilla used her powers to create small blobs of fire that floated and touched the roof of the cave.

They inspected the cave for a while and noticed that it was a bit dusty…

Max then closed his eyes and communicated with the wind. He requested the wind to collect the dust and place it in a corner of the cave.

The wind seemed to have agreed by letting a small breeze flow through the cave. The breeze collected the dust and took it out of the cave.

"Looks like the wind is your best friend…", stated Priscilla, smiling and walking around the cave, feeling the roughness of the floor of the cave.

"Yup!", replied Max, walking to the side of the cave and allowing the wind to bring in clouds.

The clouds formed a thick layer over the floor of the cave and formed bed-like structures that were soft.

Priscilla slowly seated herself over one of the beds and felt the light touch of the clouds. She smiled and looked at Max.

"Like you said, wind is my best friend.", stated Max, jumping on the second cloud and wrapping himself in the cloud blanket.

"Good night, Max...", said Priscilla, yawning.

"Good night...", reciprocated Max, slowly falling asleep from the long day they had.

3 The Next Day

The night passed by in a flash and the sun rose up in the sky with its rays reaching every part of Volmania.

The rays raced through the smallest gaps between the leaves of the trees and touched the ground. The rays landed on the leaves, helping them grow.

The forest of Volmania looked even more beautiful during day time. The light was reflected everywhere and the tree awoke.

A small patch of this landed on Axel's eyes and awoke him. Axel slowly opened his eyes looking around.

He then looked at Layla and whispered in a tired voice, "Layla… Wake up… Its morning…"

"Hmm?", questioned Layla, shedding her eyes from the light.

Layla opened her eyes, to see the exotic forest.

Although there were not many animals in sight, the plants seemed to have revealed the aura f the forest.

"Woah…", whispered Layla, mesmerized.

Axel jumped off the tree, simultaneously shapeshifting into a human. Layla did the same.

"This forest is amazing…", stated Layla, smiling.

"Nature is something magical…", said Axel, sighing.

"Yea- Wait… Did you say nature?", questioned Layla, a thought striking her head like how an arrow hits the bullseye.

"Yeah… Oh! How did we not see it before?!", exclaimed Axel, the same thought striking his head.

"The fire stone is obviously not here. What I don't understand is, why there is a forest in Volmania…", stated Layla, confused.

"It's not really here…", said Axel, scoffing.

He then snapped his finger and the forest dissolved out.

"What happened? Wasn't this the forest?", asked Layla, even more confused.

"It was an illusion. Volmania casts illusions when it feels like there might be intruders…", remarked Axel, walking back down the path they previously walked.

"Where are you going?", questioned Layla, following Axel.

"We need to go and find Max and Priscilla. The stone might be near the grassland.", replied Axel, still walking.

That's when a creature landed in front of him. The creature was black…

Layla looked concerned and approached the creature. She then asked, "Hey, are you-"

Before she could say anything else, the creature used its weapon and hit Layla with it! Layla was pushed back by the hit and she hit a tree.

Axel saw this and looked at the creature, his hands producing fire.

"Looks like it's just you and me buddy…", said Axel.

That's when ten more similar creatures landed beside the creature that hit Layla.

"Or not!", exclaimed Axel, looking at the eleven creatures.

Axel then used his powers and hit three of the creatures with bolts of fire while the other eight dodged the attack.

The three that were hit by the bolts of fire hit the ground and disappeared into thin air!

Axel then turned his gaze to the other eight and started to use his powers against them.

While fighting, one of the eight creatures flew and used an attack on Axel!

Luckily, Layla dodged it by creating a shield and retracted the attack back to the creature! The attack hit the creature and it disappeared as well!

"Hopefully, you didn't forget about me!", exclaimed Layla, smiling, using a strong water spell on about four of the remaining creatures.

"Eight down, three to go…", stated Axel, conducting electricity.

He then used the electricity on two of the creatures. The creatures got hit by the electricity and disappeared as well.

"One!", stated Layla, looking at the creature.

The creature which seemed to survive all the attacks was different. The creature worn a red coat and smiled.

The creature then transformed into a red bird with black eyes.

The creature then said, in a female voice, "Remember, this is not over. All the element stones will be ours…"

Saying this, the creature vanished.

"Where did she go?", questioned Layla, looking around.

"Some place where the others are…", replied Axel, in a serious tone.

"Others?", asked Layla, confused.

"She said 'Will be ours…'. The others who are a part of that 'ours' are at the place where she teleported.", explained Axel.

"Oh, right!", said Layla, realizing that she wasn't observant about what the creature said.

"Ahh!!", exclaimed a voice.

"What was that?!", questioned Axel.

"Sounded like…", replied Layla, thinking. "Max!"

The two teleported to the place where they first started their journey into the 'forest', and ran down the path that Priscilla and Max had taken.

They reached the place where Max and Priscilla were, which was outside the cave.

They soon burst out laughing when they saw Max.

Max didn't scream because he was hurt, he screamed because he got scared… by a tiny spider!

"Help!!", exclaimed Max, holding onto the side of the cave.

"Don't worry Max! It's just a spider…", stated Layla, sitting down on one knee in front of the spider and smiling.

The spider looked at Layla for a while and then walked away.

"See?", questioned Layla, watching Max descending down from the side of the cave.

"Yeah…", stated Max, in a low voice, watching the spider walk away.

"Did they come here as well?", asked Axel, worriedly.

"No- Wait… Who are 'they'?", questioned Priscilla, in a serious tone.

"Um… Yeah… about that…", said Layla, stuttering, looking at the wound she got when she hit the tree.

"We are all ears…", said Max, seriously.

Axel explained everything that had happened, the forest being an illusion, the creatures that attacked them, and the female creature who warned them that the element stones will be 'theirs'.

"So, you're telling us…", said Max.

"That we're being followed by some crazy creatures whose leaders want these element stones we are finding and according to what they did to you, they're willing to do anything to any-creature that comes in their way?!", questioned Max, rapidly, panicking.

"Well… when you put it in that way, it's a lot more terrifying…", stated Axel, calmly.

"It is terrifying! Oh, come on! And I was scared of a spider!", stated Max, angry.

"Then we better find that fire stone before they do!", remarked Priscilla, confidently.

The others agreed with Priscilla.

"Just one problem guys…", said Axel.

"What?", asked Layla.

"We don't know where exactly to find it.", replied Axel.

"What about the volcano?", questioned Layla,

pointing towards the volcano.

Axel replied, "Maybe, but-"

"Not the Volcano!", exclaimed Max, groaning.

"Max! We need to get the fire stone.", stated Priscilla.

"He's right actually...", added Axel.

"What?", questioned the three, in unison.

"The stone can't be at the volcano. Think about it, the creature came to us to keep us away from the fire stone. So, they might've already checked at the volcano...", stated Axel, giving an excellent reason.

"Oh, yeah... We didn't think about that part...", said Priscilla.

"So, where can the fire stone be?", questioned Max, confused.

"Well...", said Axel, thinking.

That's when they heard a huge growl...

"What was that?", questioned Priscilla, feeling the ground tremble slightly.

"Sounded like a…", stated Layla.

"Dragon!", interrupted Axel, turning around and pointing at the dragon.

"We have to calm it down… There must be something that made it furious!", stated Layla, running to the left and shapeshifting into a phoenix while jumping in the air.

"Split up!", exclaimed Layla, flying towards the dragon.

The others split up in different directions and transformed into their mythical forms.

They soon reached close to the dragon.

"Try not to hurt it… Also, don't use any fire or ice spells… They can breathe fire as well as ice…", stated Axel, analyzing the dragon's behavior.

That's when three more dragons arose and flew beside the first one.

"There's more!", exclaimed Max, panicking.

"Well, they are native to Volmania Max!",
remarked Priscilla, rapidly.

That's when the dragons spilt up and flew in front
of the four.

The four quickly spilt up in different directions,
with one dragon following them…

4 Dragons!

Layla flew southwards as fast as she could. After a while, she turned back to see if the dragon was following her.

When she did look back, she didn't see a dragon. Layla let out a sigh of relief and looked ahead.

She then spotted the dragon flying towards her! She quickly changed her course by flying upwards! That too, just in time! She flew upwards just as she was about to bump into the dragon!

Layla flew upwards for a while and reached above the surface of the clouds. She paused in one place, taking a breath. Just then, the dragon appeared!

Layla quickly analyzed the dragon in a few seconds while the dragon searched the other side of the clouds.

She then concluded that it was a silver dragon. Layla then remembered what her mother told her about silver dragons! That silver dragons enjoy the company of humans and elves.

Then she remembered what Axel told her about

silver dragons.

"Axel told me that silver dragons have silver eyes…", thought Layla to herself. "This dragon has… black eyes…"

That's when she remembered something else. She looked below the clouds by pulling a small part of the cloud apart. She soon noticed that see had travelled to an entirely opposite part of Volmania. This part was full of snow-clad mountains.

She then noticed that she made a terrible mistake…

That's when she looked at the dragon, and noticed a cold wave of air gushing towards her. Just as she tried to fly, the cold wave of air hit her and displaced her about 2 km away from her previous position.

She then stood on her feet on the clouds and looked at the dragon, who was speedily growing in size as he came closer.

That's when an idea struck her mind. She quickly teleported to where she previously was before the dragon hit her with the cold air. She then started to fly downwards towards the snow-clad mountains.

~

Meanwhile, Max flew above one of the dragons and headed northwards, with the dragon following him.

Max looked back and noticed that it was a copper dragon.

"A copper dragon?", thought Max to himself, looking ahead and focused on where he was flying. "Aren't those the dragons which Priscilla mentioned earlier? She said I would get along with them pretty well… I never asked why…"

That's when the dragon huffed a gush of air out of its nose and used its mouth to release a gas…

The gas came in contact with Max. Max sniffed the gas and coughed and looked back and stated, "How old are you buddy?"

That's when Max realized something… He was slower than before!

He flapped his wings faster, however, failed to increase his speed!

The copper dragon closed in and Max stopped flapping his wings! He dropped down into the thick forest situated below…

The copper dragon huffed and landed on the ground where there were fewer trees.

Max was hiding among the trees far away from the dragon and was steadily progressing to exit the forest and stay away from the dragon…

~

Priscilla flew eastwards without thinking too much and sped away!

She looked back to find an Electrum dragon! She remembered about their powers and built a shield around herself just in time.

She looked back once again and didn't see the dragon. She looked ahead and noticed the Electrum dragon sitting…

"Hello…", said the Electrum dragon, in a deep voice.

"Hello?", questioned Priscilla, looking around.

"I know you know that I am controlled by another creature… However, no control spell can take away my trading personality away from me… So, if you trade with me, I shall resist the control spell as much as I can…", stated the Electrum dragon, polishing its nails.

"But a trade works two ways… So, you have to give me something I want as well…", stated Priscilla seating herself in front of the dragon.

"Hmm… I sense that you're the clever one… However, I am already offering to resist the spell, so one part of the deal is sealed…

The one that remains is yours…", replied the Electrum dragon.

"Name it, you get it.", replied Priscilla, smiling and transforming into a human.

That's when the Electrum dragon realized something…

He then stated, "I would like to have… that…"

Priscilla followed the direction in which the dragon pointed and noticed what the dragon wanted…

It was her ruby necklace which was gifted to her by someone!

"Anything, BUT the necklace", added Priscilla, holding onto the necklace.

"Hmm... Very well... Seems that the necklace is very valuable to you...

How about this... You can ask for something from me that you think will be as valuable as that ruby necklace... I will give you what you want, as well as resist the spell...", replied the Electrum dragon.

"Uh- Ok... I would like you to use your healing powers to remove the spell casted on you...", replied Priscilla.

The Electrum dragon was surprised to hear this response. He expected that Priscilla would ask for something that she required... The dragon didn't expect Priscilla to care about the control spell...

"I see... Anything else?", questioned the dragon, wisely.

"You said anything however I thought it would only be one thing.", stated Priscilla, confused.

"I may like the necklace but I also like a FAIR trade. So, I allow you to ask for anything else once again...", replied the dragon, smiling.

"Ok... I would also like to know the location of the air element stone...", replied Priscilla, smiling.

"Very well... I shall first have the necklace and then I shall give you my part of the trade...", said the dragon, keeping his palm in front of Priscilla.

Priscilla took the necklace off and looked at it for the last time and sighed. She passed the necklace over to the dragon, who kept the necklace beside it.

The dragon closed its eyes and used its healing powers to end the control spell casted on it! The dragon was successful in doing so!

The dragon stretched for a while and then turned to Priscilla and said, "Now, for the location of the air element stone...

It is located in Galesia."

"Galesia?", questioned Priscilla, trying to recall the name.

"It is a dimension which is full of different creatures. You may come across many false paths, however, remember to choose the one which seems least expected...

Galesia knows how to protect herself… Either with the help of her creatures, or, by herself…", replied the Electrum dragon, in a serious tone.

"How do we reach Galesia?", asked Priscilla.

"My part of the trade was only to tell you the location, not how to reach the location…", stated the Electrum dragon.

"That ruby necklace was very valuable to me… Nothing can replace it for me… So, I think you can give me one more thing I need…", said Priscilla, in a low yet stern voice.

The Electrum dragon thought about this for a while and nodded.

"Only a creature associated with Galesia's creatures can open a portal there… Even if you open a portal there, the portal may… break out, or malfunction and result in leading you to an undesired location…", replied the Electrum dragon.

"Undesired location? That would mean maybe the locations we are associated with…", stated Priscilla.

"Incorrect. That can be a possibility with less than 2% chances of occurring. The undesired location can be any random dimension...", stated the Electrum dragon.

"Oh... Ok...", said Priscilla. She then heard the thud sound and looked in the direction of the sound. She saw that the copper dragon which had followed Max was searching the forest thoroughly.

"I need to leave...", said Priscilla, looking at the dragon.

The dragon nodded and smiled.

Priscilla smiled back and jumped off the rock she was previously sitting on and transformed into a phoenix and flew towards the forest...

~

Axel, on the other hand, travelled towards the active volcano with a gold dragon following him.

He headed to the volcano and paused to look at the gold dragon. The gold dragon paused in front of him and Axel looked directly into its eyes.

His fingers then glowed with fire and he slowly placed his hand on the gold dragon…

The gold dragon stood calm and closed its eyes.

The energy from Axel's finger flowed through the gold dragon. After a while, the dragon opened its eyes and looked around. Then, the dragon turned its gaze towards Axel.

"Thank you…", said the gold dragon, smiling.

"You remember what happened? Who did this to you?!", questioned Axel, hurriedly.

"I sense that you need to be somewhere near the snow-clad mountains to help a friend of yours. My friend, the silver dragon, is being controlled… It was some bird who was red in color and had black eyes who put us under the control spell…", replied the gold dragon, rapidly.

"Wait… Red bird- Never mind! I need to help Layla! Thank you for your help!!", exclaimed Axel, jumping and transforming into a phoenix.

Axel flew rapidly towards the snow-clad mountains…

Meanwhile, Priscilla reached the forest where she had previously spotted the dragon. She then shapeshifted into a human and walked through the forest, looking for Max, with caution.

She soon spotted Max and waved at him. Max waved back and rushed towards Priscilla without making a sound.

Soon, Priscilla realized something terrible about Max's hand.

"What happened? You're hurt so badly...", whispered Priscilla, looking at the 3 scratches on Max's hand.

Max himself was shocked when he saw the scratches.

"Must've happened when I fell. The branches must've scratched me...", whispered back Max, looking at his arm.

"Let's go... We can't stay here...", said Priscilla, still whispering.

"But where?", questioned Max.

Priscilla looked at the volcano and spotted the gold dragon that had followed Axel!

"There! The gold dragon may be able to tell us where Axel is…", stated Priscilla, pointing at the dragon.

"Don't you remember, the dragons are being controlled!", stated Max, looking at the copper dragon, who was searching for Max vigorously.

"Then where's Axel? And Layla! She headed south, didn't she?", questioned Priscilla, trying to recall as much as she could, looking at Max.

"Yes! We should go south as well then!", stated Max. "But what if Axel is still dealing with the gold dragon? Shouldn't we go and help him?"

Priscilla looked back at the gold dragon, who was quietly sitting on the rock next to the volcano…

"I think we're good. Axel seems to have done something to the dragon. The gold dragon is pretty calm…", remarked Priscilla, looking at the dragon.

"Then let's go! It's only going to be a few more minutes till the copper dragon will have searched this entire forest!", stated Max, looking at the copper dragon.

"Isn't that Axel?", questioned Max, looking at the fire globe that was steadily aiming towards the snow-clad mountains.

"It is!", replied Priscilla. "I'll teleport us to the mountains!"

Priscilla snapped her fingers and the two were teleported to the outskirts of the mountains.

Max looked up and spotted Axel. He noticed that Axel was already deep into the interiors of the mountains.

"Wow! He's pretty fast!", stated Max, impressed by Axel's speed.

"Let's go in!", mentioned Priscilla, snapping her fingers and giving Max and herself warm clothes.

"You surely did think of everything…", stated Max, rushing into the interiors of the mountains with Priscilla by his side.

~

The Mystery of the Element Stones

Layla was flying towards the snow-clad mountains slowly…

The ice in the air formed icicles on her wings and seemed weighed her down…

After a while, Layla couldn't fly! She started to descend towards the ground rapidly!

Within a few seconds, she landed on the snow. Luckily, the snow softened her landing…

Layla tried to help herself up. That's when she heard a familiar voice!

"Layla!!", called out Axel.

"I'm here!", called back Layla, trying to move her wings.

Axel followed the direction of the voice instinctively and spotted Layla.

"What happened?", questioned Axel, transforming into a human and examining Layla's wings.

"The ice… It froze my wings… That's why I crash landed…", replied Layla.

Axel took a deep breath and blew a small amount of fire from his mouth onto Layla's wings…

The fire quickly melted the ice and Layla's wings were good as new!

"How'd you do that?", questioned Layla, surprised.

Axel was about to answer and that when he pushed Layla aside and jumped in the same direction.

Layla transformed into a human and noticed a huge ball of ice crashing where she was.

She looked up and spotted… the silver dragon!

"We have to go to!", exclaimed Layla, transforming into a phoenix and flying towards the mountains.

"Where?!", questioned Axel, transforming into a phoenix and looking at the dragon.

The dragon paused and stared at Axel. Axel slowly raised his hand and a small glow was emitted…

He slowly placed his palm on the dragon and let the energy flow through the dragon.

The dragon absorbed the energy and closed its eyes.

Layla looked back and noticed what Axel was doing. She paused and decided to see what happens…

That's when a deep voice spoke from within the dragon.

"I have already failed to find the fire element, I won't fail in finding it again!", exclaimed the voice.

As soon as the deep voice completed its sentence, the dragon broke out of the energy that Axel provided it! Axel was thrown down to the snowy ground due the power of the energy!

Layla's eyes grew small as she saw Axel crash-land on the snowy ground.

She then looked at the dragon, who was presently gazing at Priscilla and Max.

Layla gesticulated towards Priscilla and Max to

distract the dragon.

Priscilla and Max nodded and transformed into their mythical forms and started the diversion.

Layla sat down on the ground beside Axel and helped him up.

"That was a powerful negative aura... The silver dragon can't break through the control spell...", stated Axel, looking at the dragon.

"Follow me! We don't know how long Priscilla and Max can distract that dragon...", remarked Layla, flying towards the mountains.

Axel nodded and followed Layla into the mountains.

After a while, the two reached the mountains circle and noticed several more silver dragons interacting and laughing.

Layla landed on the snow and transformed into a human. Axel followed.

Axel then stated, "We need your help! One of the silver dragons is being controlled!"

"Controlled? That's impossible... No silver dragon left the blizzard circle...", replied one of the silver dragons, walking towards Layla and Axel.

"There must be one! The silver dragon had a negative aura...", remarked Layla, insistent.

"One dragon did leave...", stated another silver dragon, looking at the first silver dragon.

"Anthony! Now I remember... He told us that he was leaving to meet his friends!", exclaimed the first silver dragon.

"Can you please help us? We heard you have healing powers...", stated Axel.

"We do... However, out of all the healing spells, only the Amorfian spell has worked for powerful magic...", replied the second silver dragon.

"I already used that spell. The creature who is controlling Anthony is very powerful...", added Axel.

"The Amorfian spell? That spell is only known to the silver dragons... May I ask how you know that spell...", questioned the first dragon.

"I will answer that question later... But right now, we have to cut off the control spell...", stated Axel, hurriedly.

"We won't be able to break the spell, but we can try to weaken its effect. The weakening won't be in a large quantity, but it's the best option...", stated the second dragon.

"Then let's go!", exclaimed Layla, flying out of the blizzard circle.

The dragons nodded and Axel and all the 18 dragons followed Layla.

After a while, the two and the 18 dragons reached the destination.

However, Layla and Axel were petrified!

The silver dragon that was being controlled had seemed to have used very powerful spells on Priscilla and Max.

Priscilla and Max were barely able to maintain their balance.

Layla fired up with fury and landed in front of

Anthony.

She then builds a shield around Priscilla and Max and turned to Anthony.

Layla then used an ice spell on Anthony!

"Layla, not ice!", exclaimed Axel, watching the other 18 dragons land beside Layla.

Layla then witnessed Anthony breathe in the spell and grow stronger!

That's when she remembered that silver dragons can breathe ice!

The other 18 dragons started to weaken the control spell while Layla and Axel healed Priscilla and Max.

"Don't…", said Max. "hurt the dragon…"

"Don't worry… The other dragons are only weakening the control spell…", replied Axel.

"That's even worse! Why do you think Priscilla and I are so weak! We both used the most powerful spells we knew and the dragon seemed to have absorbed our spells and used them on us!", exclaimed Max, looking outside the shield.

Axel and Layla looked outside the shield as well and found only one silver dragon weakening the control spell.

"Anthony's still under the control spell…", uttered Layla.

Axel flew out of the shield and stood in front of Anthony.

The other silver dragon had fallen unconscious…

Axel then closed his eyes and prepared a fire attack and shot it towards Anthony!

When the fire hit Anthony, it flew past him, taking away the remnants of the control spell with it.

The dark magic faded out of Anthony and Axel huffed and puffed.

Anthony looked around and was devastated… All the silver dragons were unconscious, with no energy or power…

Axel took a deep breath and released ice onto all

the dragons...

The dragons breathed in the ice and stood up. They looked at Anthony, and noticed that he was free from the control spell!

The silver dragons rejoiced and thanked the four for their help in bringing back Anthony and recovering them from the effect of the powerful spells used on them.

Layla smiled and stated, "It was all Axel. He was the one who broke that control spell and recovered all of you."

"Thank you, Axel...", stated one of the silver dragons, smiling.

"Indeed... You have helped us all...", added... the gold dragon!

The gold dragon was accompanied by the other dragons that the four had helped!

"We are forever indebted to you. You have broken a very powerful spell...", stated the Electrum dragon, smiling.

The Electrum dragon turned to Priscilla and

opened his palm in front of her.

Priscilla's ruby necklace lay in the enormous palm of the Electrum dragon.

"I believe that this belongs to you...", said the Electrum dragon, wisely.

"But... I thought we traded it...", stated Priscilla, confused.

"You traded the necklace?", questioned Max.

"I had to... The situation was such...", replied Priscilla.

"You four have helped us a lot, and I believe that this necklace is something I can give to you as a Thank You...", added the Electrum dragon.

Priscilla smiled and picked up the necklace. She then wore the necklace carefully around her neck, with the ruby shining brightly.

Suddenly, a loud growl was heard... The ground trembled and a large sound was heard!

"What is that?", questioned Max, holding onto Priscilla.

"The volcano!", exclaimed Axel, transforming into a phoenix and heading out of the snow-clad mountains at the speed of light!

Layla, Max and Priscilla followed Axel instinctively.

After a while of flying, they arrived at the active Volcano.

That's when they noticed something! Axel was flying around the volcano, preventing the lava to flow down.

The three looked at the bottom of the Volcano, and noticed that about 37 dragons were asleep there!

"Let's wake those sleepy-heads!", stated Priscilla, flying over to the dragons.

Layla and Max nodded and they started to wake the dragons.

After a few minutes, they managed to evacuate all the area at the bottom of the Volcano.

That's when the Volcano growled again and the three turned their gaze towards Axel.

Axel was a human, yet he was not being burnt by the lava, heat and flames.

That's when Layla spotted Axel wearing a ring! She looked at it carefully and concluded that it's the fire element stone!

"He's bonded with the fire element!", exclaimed the copper dragon.

Axel landed on the ground and smiled.

Priscilla came forward and mentioned, "A friend of mine told me that the air element stone is in Galesia…"

"Then let's go there!", exclaimed Layla, excitedly.

"Yeah!", exclaimed Max, flying vigorously in loops.

The three chuckled as they saw Max looping around the dragons…

5 Galesia

The four took their leave and walked back to the place where Axel had first teleported them.

"Volmania is so… amazing…", stated Layla, looking at the dragons.

"Yeah!", exclaimed Max, looking back. "Except the volcano…"

Layla, Priscilla and Axel chuckled and after a while they reached their destination.

"Wait! I forgot to mention one detail…", stated Priscilla. "Only a creature associated with Galesia can open a portal to Galesia…"

"Well, we could try to create a portal…", suggested Layla.

"We can't. The electrum dragon mentioned that if we try to create a portal to Galesia, Galesia will use her powers to divert the portal to an undesired location… And that undesired destination can be anywhere…"

"Well…", stated Axel, thinking. "Galesia is the wind dimension… So…" Axel looked at Max.

"Why are you looking at me?", questioned Max, worriedly.

"You're a hippogriff! You could try to open a portal!", exclaimed Axel, smiling.

"I've never created a portal… The only way I could open a portal was using the hippogriff's gem…", reminded Max, calmly.

"Maybe you could use your wind powers?", questioned Layla, stepping forward.

"I could, but how will I create a portal with wind?", asked Max, bringing a light breeze.

"Maybe think about where you want to go and imagine a portal… That works for phoenixes…", suggested Priscilla.

Max thought about it for a while, and then nodded.

He stepped forward and took a deep breath…

He raised his hands and whistled a low tune.

A breeze started to flow slowly yet steadily.

As every second passed, the breeze converted into a tornado…

Soon, a portal was starting to form… But… It was too strong!

"I can't… control… it…", stated Max, his hands trembling.

As soon as Max said this, Priscilla was sucked into the portal.

"Priscilla!", exclaimed Layla, holding onto Axel, who was himself struggling to hold onto a boulder.

Max soon lost complete control of the portal and he too was sucked into it!

"We need to go in it!", exclaimed Axel, looking at Layla.

Layla nodded and let go of Axel and allowed herself to fall into the portal. Axel smiled and fell back into the portal as well.

~

The four fell out of the portal in a completely different dimension.

Max got up and looked around.

"Woah...", stated Max, looking around.

Priscilla and Layla got up as well and gazed around in awe...

Meanwhile, Axel was stuck to the ground!

"Guys... I'm a little...", stated Axel, pulling himself. "Stuck..."

"Huh?", questioned Priscilla, confused.

"Yeah... I don't know if it's just me being... lazy... But I am stuck...", added Axel, still struggling to get up.

Layla walked over to Axel, and held his arm. She then pulled with all her might, however, in vain.

"It's definitely not you being lazy... Priscilla, Max, can you help me?", questioned Layla.

Priscilla and Max nodded and the three pulled with all their strength. But Axel was still glued to the ground.

"You can't set him free...", stated a voice.

"What?", questioned Layla, confused.

"You can't set him free!", repeated a pixie.

"Why is that so?", asked Priscilla, skeptical.

"Because Galesia protects herself! She uses her powers to stop creatures from hurting her creatures...", replied the pixie.

"Do you know how we can free him?", questioned Max.

"Yup!", exclaimed the pixie. "But I can't tell you... It's usually a Galesian secret... And I am too young to perform that powerful spell..."

"Wait... If Galesia protects herself from other creatures, why aren't Priscilla and I stuck?", questioned Layla.

"Priscilla is a princess! And you're a human! That's why!", replied the pixie, playfully.

"Wait... You know us?", questioned Priscilla,

confused.

"Of course, we do! You're the creatures who brought back peace at the Enchanted Forest!", stated the pixie, smiling.

"Um… Guys… I am still stuck…", reminded Axel, lazily.

"How do we free Axel if we don't even know the galesian secret?", questioned Priscilla, looking at the pixie.

"Maybe he can do it…", said the pixie, pointing at Max.

Max looked around and then pointed at himself and questioned, "Me?!"

"Yup!", added the pixie, doing air loops.

"How can you be so sure?", asked Max, confused.

"Galesian gut…", added the pixie, smiling.

"Ok… But how do I free him if I don't know anything about the spell?", questioned Max, looking at the pixie which seemed to have an answer for everything.

"That! You need to figure out!", exclaimed the pixie.

Max looked dissatisfied with the answer and groaned.

"Can you please tell us which creature can tell us the spell?", asked Priscilla, confident that the pixie had an answer.

"Hmm… Maybe you can ask the plants to help you?", stated the pixie.

"Maybe… Thank you for your help.", stated Priscilla, kindly.

Max was shocked that Priscilla got an answer out of the very secretive pixie.

The pixie smiled cheerfully and turned to fly away.

"Wait!", called out Layla, thinking.

"Yes?", questioned the pixie.

"Do you by any chance, know a pixie named Moon?", asked Layla, hopefully.

"Of course, I do! She's the leader of the pixie clan!", exclaimed the pixie, flying upside down.

"What?!", questioned the four, with Axel still stuck to the ground.

"You heard it right. You could visit her now if you want.", stated the pixie.

"It would be amazing to see Moon after such a long time...", said Priscilla, taking a short yet amazing walk down memory lane.

"How do you guys know the leader of the pixie clan?", asked Axel, baffled.

"Long story short, she was with us for a short time back at Layla's home, before the night we met you.", replied Max.

"Oh!", exclaimed Axel.

"Do you know her?", questioned Priscilla.

"Yup! She's my childhood friend!", stated Axel.

"Woah! How many creatures do you know?", questioned Max, his head rotating.

"Many… I like to explore…", replied Axel, trying to pull his right arm free.

"Don't try to free yourself. It will only get you stuck more!", stated the pixie.

"No wonder I feel more glued to the ground…", murmured Axel, resting.

Layla pulled Priscilla and Max aside. She looked around and noticed they were out of earshot.

Layla recalled, "Maybe Moon can help us… Remember, the night we met Axel, we were at home before. When we were-"

"Eavesdropping?", questioned Priscilla and Max in union.

"I wouldn't call it 'eavesdropping'… But, when we were listening to great granny Emma and Moon's conversation, Moon seemed to know a lot about magic and the banishment spell… Probably she knows the solution to getting Axel unstuck…", concluded Layla.

"True… Maybe she can perform the spell…", added Priscilla.

"Quick question! Why am I not stuck to the ground like Axel? We know why you guys are not stuck…", questioned Max.

"Because… You the prince of the hippogriffs and you are a creature related to wind…", replied Priscilla.

"Oh, right!", stated Max. "Go on."

"Well, we can't leave Axel here alone… He seems pretty tired as well from being stuck…", stated Layla.

"Maybe Priscilla and I can go visit Moon and you can stay here…", suggested Max.

"Okay! Sounds like a plan!", stated Layla and Priscilla, in unison.

Max and Priscilla transformed into their mythical forms and were ready to take off.

"Can you please guide us to Moon?", requested Priscilla.

"Sure!", exclaimed the pixie, flapping her wings faster.

"Great! Then let's take off!", exclaimed Max, flying.

Priscilla nodded and jumped to take flight. But she fell down!

"Priscilla! Are you okay?", questioned Layla, helping her up along with Max.

"Yeah...", replied Priscilla, trying to take flight again.

However, she fell again! Luckily, she landed on her claws this time.

"Why am I not able to fly?", questioned Priscilla, flapping her wings vigorously while she stood on the ground.

"I forgot to mention... Galesia may allow you to walk, but she can't allow you use certain abilities... I guess she took your ability to fly...", stated the pixie, in a low voice, sitting on Priscilla's back.

"I guess I'll walk. This is going to be a long... walk...", stated Priscilla, looking at all the hills, while transforming into a human.

"You can hop onto my back! I am strong! Plus, I can fly!", suggested Max, standing in front of Priscilla.

Priscilla looked confused.

"I'm not taking no for an answer!", exclaimed Max, helping Priscilla up.

"Okay… Thank you Max…", said Priscilla, hopping onto Max's back.

"Let's go!", exclaimed the pixie, flying towards the hills.

"Yeah!", exclaimed Max, taking flight, flying fast.

Layla waved bye as the Priscilla, Max and the pixie grew small in size.

There was silence for a while… Layla sat down beside the stuck Axel.

"I've been thinking about something for a while now…", stated Axel, breaking the silence.

"Hm?", questioned Layla.

"You remember that creature we met? In the fake

forest?", questioned Axel, in a low voice.

Layla then recalled the terrible wound she got from that time…

"Yeah…", replied Layla.

"I feel that the creature might come here…", added Axel.

"Maybe… What if they're the Dark Creature, the one that Katherine Loophole mentioned?", asked Layla, a shiver running down her spine.

"That would make sense. I mean, the creature we met did say 'we', and was stern about her decision of finding the elements…", stated Axel, thinking deeply.

"Then… wouldn't that mean… she's here right now?!", questioned Layla, getting up, panicking.

"That pixie! That must've been that creature! That means Max and Priscilla are in danger!", exclaimed Axel, trying to get up.

"We need to get you unstuck now!", exclaimed Layla, walking around, panicking.

"Even if that pixie was the creature we met before, we know that she wasn't lying about me bring stuck and the spell getting tighter! And, now that I think carefully, the pixie can't be the creature we met. Remember what the pixie said? Galesia protects herself!", stated Axel.

"What if you're stuck, not because of Galesia's spell, but because that creature casted a spell on you? Think about it! I am part-human part-phoenix, and yet Galesia didn't cast a spell on me when I am a creature who is not related to wind!", exclaimed Layla.

"Right! The creature thought of all possible ways to keep us from using any kind of spell, because she knew that we'd be able to break it!", stated Axel.

"Which spell should I use though? I am still not well-versed with them…", stated Layla, confused.

"I'll guide you. Try and use…", said Axel, thinking. "Affirmitia-reversa…"

"Um…", said Layla, baffled.

Axel let out a sigh and stated, "Just, place your palm of my arm and say, 'Affirmitia-Reversa!'", stated Axel.

"*Oh, okay!*", exclaimed Layla.

"*Remember, don't pronounce it wrong...*", warned Axel.

"*Why? I mean, usually if we pronounce a spell wrong, nothing happens. Right?*", confirmed Layla, curious.

"*Those are basic spells. Spells like these ones sound very similar to other spells... If you say 'Affir-MA-tia' instead of 'Affir-MI-tia', it could change the effect of the spell...*", replied Axel, trying to pull his arm.

"*What will happen if I say 'Affir-MA-tia'?*", asked Layla, worriedly.

"*I don't want to know...*", stated Axel, a shiver running down his spine.

"*Ok... Let's do it!*", said Layla, placing her palm on Axel's arm.

Layla took a deep breath and chanted, "*Affirmitia-Reversa!*"

She looked at Axel, but he was still stuck... She retrieved her palm and stood up.

Axel pulled his arm and the suction which pulled him released him!

Axel soon got up and smiled.

"You're unstuck!", exclaimed Layla, relieved.

"Luckily you chanted it correctly…", stated Axel, stretching his arms.

"I am amazing at following instructions.", added Layla, proudly.

Axel looked around and said, "Come on! We don't have much time until-"

Layla pushed Axel aside and the two dodged a fireball attack!

Layla looked at the source, and stated, "Looks like we have visitors!"

"Element…Stones…", uttered a creature in red, with black eyes.

"Now we can be sure that the pixie was the creature we met in Volmania!", stated Axel, launching an electric attack at the creatures.

The three creatures that stood in front of them were hit by the attack, but they managed to sustain it!

"These creatures are different from the ones we met in Volmania.", added Layla, dodging a water attack.

"How?", asked Axel, flying in his human form, with the help of his element stone. "They look the same to me…"

"That's the thing! They look the same!", exclaimed Layla, backflipping to dodge an attack from the creature. "They are more powerful! Look at their eyes carefully!"

Axel caught hold of a creature when the creature started to attack him. He gazed at the creature's eyes and noticed something… Their pupils were shaped like staffs!

"You're right!", exclaimed Axel, using a fire attack on the creature he had previously caught hold of.

Layla ran towards a creature and used a water wave attack on it. The creature was pushed into the air, but it landed on its feet a few meters away!

"How do we stop these though?!", questioned Layla, watching the creature coming in close from where it had landed.

"Maybe try using their own attack on them!", answered Axel, observing one of the creatures preparing a fire attack.

The creature released the fire attack towards Axel. Axel caught hold of the attack and reversed its direction and threw it towards the creature.

"Like that!", added Axel, observing that the creature disappeared.

"Got it!", replied Layla, catching hold of a water attack and enhancing its power. She then threw the attack towards the creature and the creature was pushed into a portal by the water attack!

"Woah! How'd you get that portal there?", questioned Axel, fascinated.

"I didn't!", replied Layla, confused.

They noticed that there was only one of the creatures left! But they didn't have to do anything.

A gush of wind carried the creature with it and

soon send it through a portal!

"What was that?", questioned Layla, surprised.

"A Sylph!", exclaimed Axel.

"A… Sylph?", questioned Layla, confused, looking at the gush of wind that twirled.

"It's a wind spirit which is native only to Galesia. It has the control over the wind and sky.", replied Axel, rapidly.

"Oh…", said Layla, mesmerized by the sylph.

Layla and Axel thanked the sylph and the sylph disappeared into its natural form.

"Let's go! Who knows where Max and Priscilla are!", exclaimed Axel, flying towards the dense forest.

"Right behind you!", exclaimed Layla, flying.

~

Meanwhile, Max and Priscilla had reached deep into the forest with the pixie.

After a while, Max looked around and whispered to Priscilla, "This isn't how a pixie village is supposed to look like, right?"

"No… I feel like this pixie is someone else…", whispered back Priscilla.

Max slowed down his pace, thinking that the pixie might hear them.

"We should go back…", whispered Priscilla, watching the pixie.

Max nodded and turned around to fly back.

"Where do you think you're going?", questioned the pixie, her hand glowing.

Max heard this and sped away. But soon he was pushed by some kind of barrier!

"You thought I wouldn't know that you knew I wasn't a pixie?", questioned the pixie, landing on the ground.

"Um… Actually, we didn't think that…", replied Max, shrugging his shoulders.

"Oh! Guess you didn't know about them.",

questioned the pixie, pointing to her left and right.

That's when three dark creatures landed behind her! The pixie glowed and broke! Soon, a creature appeared!

"You! You're the one who met Axel and Layla in Volmania!", exclaimed Priscilla, recalling the description Layla gave them about the creature.

"Oh, I am well-known? That's nice to hear…", stated the creature, smiling. "One more thing, my name is not 'creature', my name is Scarlett."

"Well, at least the name suits you…", remarked Max, looking at the red coat around Scarlett.

Scarlett smiled and commanded, "They're your job now boys!"

Saying that, Scarlett transformed into her bird form and took off.

The creatures that stood behind Scarlett, looked at Max and Priscilla, and their eyes grew red…

"That's not good.", stated Priscilla, jumping on the ground.

The creatures rushed towards Max and Priscilla and used a combined water spell on them. This enhanced the spell's power a lot and Max and Priscilla were pushed back by it through the dense forest.

One of the creatures prepared a fire attack and shot it towards Max and Priscilla. Max got up and used his power to send the attack back to the creature. He reversed the direction of the flow of wind by a great amount that the attack was stuck in one place as it tried to resist the effect of the wind.

After a few seconds, the wind pushed the attack back to its source and the creature disappeared.

However, by that time, another creature already released a lava attack towards Max! The other creature was fighting with Priscilla.

The lava attack was caught hold off and it was reversed back to the creature. The creature sustained it, however, was pushed aback.

"Need a hand?", questioned Axel, smiling.

"Yes!", exclaimed Priscilla, dodging every punch that the other creature shot at her.

"Layla and I'll take care of that one!", stated Axel, pointing at the creature which was stuck in the trees.

"I'll go help Priscilla!", stated Max, rushing towards the creature that was fighting with Priscilla.

Max gesticulated a sign to Priscilla within a second and Priscilla nodded. Max used his powers to call the sylph.

The sylph arrived and followed the direction in which Max directed his hands. It carried the creature upward.

Priscilla smiled and used her powers to grow weeds that caught hold of the creature. The weeds grew around the creature and held it tightly.

The creature was then pushed into a portal by the weeds. The portal was created by the sylph who was helping them.

Max had told the sylph about the portal by the movement of his hands!

"Just you and us, buddy. Right Layla?",

questioned Axel, smiling, preparing a fire attack.

But he received no response… Axel looked back and questioned, "Layla?"

He was shocked to see that Layla was nowhere in sight! She was not with Max and Priscilla, or anywhere in the forest.

That's when he was hit by the creature that remained! He was then pushed back by the attack and landed a few feet away.

"Axel! Are you okay?", questioned Max.

"I am. But I am not sure if Layla is.", replied Axel, getting up.

"What do you mean?", questioned Priscilla, forming a shield around themselves.

"Layla isn't here and the last time I saw her was at the plains, where we fought a few of these creatures as well.", stated Axel. "Max, try and find Layla with the help of the sylph. We'll ward off this creature."

Max nodded and closed his eyes. He then opened them, having completely white eyes.

"Let Max be in the shield.", stated Axel, jumping out off the shield and using a lava attack on the creature, that pushed it back.

Priscilla nodded and minimized the size of the shield so that only Max could fit in it. She then rushed out to help Axel with the creature.

Meanwhile, Max used his mind to communicate with the sylph. He whispered, "Slyph of Galesia, help me find Layla Woods…"

The sylph heard this request and rushed out of the forest and searched Galesia thoroughly. Soon, the sylph told Max Layla's exact location!

"Guys, the sylph's found Layla!", exclaimed Max, his eyes turning back to normal.

Axel and Priscilla nodded.

Axel looked at the creature and smiled.

"Don't worry, Priscilla will keep you company.", stated Axel, teleporting him and Max to the plains.

Priscilla rose weeds and ferns from the ground and said, "Hopefully, you love weeds!"

The Mystery of the Element Stones

(Created by me)

She then sent the weeds in the direction of the creature.

~

Axel and Max followed the sylph back to the plains where Axel and Layla had previously been.

They landed at a spot where the sylph disappeared and they looked around.

"Layla's not here…", murmured Axel, worriedly.

"Hi guys…", said Layla, standing behind Axel and Max.

"Phew! You're safe!", exclaimed Axel, reliefed.

"Of course, I am! Why did you think I wasn't safe?", questioned Layla, confused.

"Well, the creature you guys met at Volmania met us at the forest! That's why! And her name's Scarlett.", informed Max, briefing everything.

"Oh…", said Layla.

That's when Axel noticed something… Layla still had the scar she got at the illusional forest in

Volmania. The weird part was that the scar was glowing blue brightly…

Axel looked around, making sure that Layla didn't notice him. Then he turned his gaze to Layla and said, "Layla?"

"Hm?", questioned Layla, smiling.

"Forgive me later if you can…", stated Axel.

Layla looked confused and asked, "For-"

Axel threw a lava ball towards Layla, which pushed her about a few miles away!

"Axel! Why'd you do that?", questioned Max, furious at what Axel had done.

Axel looked at the smoke carefully and then noticed something.

"Just like I thought!", stated Axel, conducting electricity.

"What?", questioned Max, gazing at the smoke.

That's when he too saw what the smoke revealed. It was… Scarlett.

Scarlett teleported in front of Axel and Max and stated, "You're pretty observant…"

"Where's Layla?", asked Max, prepared to use his powers.

"Oh! She was here a while ago. Too bad, YOU didn't notice your friend getting caught!", replied Scarlett, pointing towards Axel.

Axel soon realized what had happened…

"While you were flying into the forest, one of my friends seemed to have caught hold of Layla…", stated Scarlett.

That's when one of the dark creatures landed on the ground, with its arm extended to hold… Layla.

"Layla!", exclaimed Axel and Max, in unison.

Layla however mumbled a few words.

"Oh, she won't say anything…", stated Scarlett.

"Lock-jaw spell…", uttered Axel, feeling guilty that it was his fault that Layla was captured.

Max quickly shot a wind attack towards the creature's arm that forced it to let go of Layla.

Layla landed on her feet and immediately used her powers to trap the creature in ice.

Scarlett looked at the creature trapped in ice and flew in the air.

"Won't take me long to find that wind element stone!", exclaimed Scarlett.

Axel looked at Layla, who was trying to catch her breath.

Axel shot a small spell at Layla's mouth which altered the lock-jaw spell.

Layla opened her mouth and caught a breath. She then turned to Axel and Max and said, "Thanks Guys…"

"I'm so… sorry…", uttered Axel, devastated.

"What… do you mean?", questioned Layla, confused.

"If I had paid more attention, you wouldn't have been caught…", replied Axel.

Layla tried comforted Axel and said, "Well, I told you to go ahead and I was going to follow you and-"

"Still! I was with you the whole time and I just, sped away...", interrupted Axel.

Max then changed the subject unknowingly and recalled something!

"Priscilla! We need to go!", exclaimed Max, speeding towards the forest.

Axel and Layla nodded and they followed Max back to the forest.

When they reached the forest, they found the dark creature and Priscilla.

However, the dark creature was now wound up tightly in weeds and ferns!

"Wow! You guys came back quick!", stated Priscilla, surprised.

"Woah... How did you do that?", questioned Max, looking at the dark creature trying to use all its strength to break through the weeds.

"Something I learnt myself…", replied Priscilla, proudly.

The creature then disappeared into thin air.

"I didn't even hold him that tightly… Why'd he disappear?", questioned Priscilla, retrieving the weeds and ferns.

"Maybe he was called back?", questioned Max, thoughtfully.

"Called… Back?", asked Layla, confused.

"Think about it. Scarlett was technically commanding these creatures… She might have called this one back using her powers…", replied Max.

"That might be possible.", stated Priscilla.

That's when Axel recalled something terrible.

"We need to go!", exclaimed Axel. "Scarlett mentioned that she is going to find the air element stone!"

"Right!", added Max, taking off.

Layla and Priscilla sensed trouble and they and Axel followed Max out of the forest.

Max called out to the sylph and communicated with her, and briefed her about the danger that would occur if they didn't stop Scarlett.

The sylph communicated back and told Max to follow her.

They soon reached an empty part of another forest. The sylph then took her true form and stated, "You can take this element stone, and return it back to me, once Galesia is safe."

The air element stone rose up in the sky and flew over to Max's hoof.

Max smiled and sylph disappeared into her wind form.

"Let's go!", exclaimed Max, flying out of the forest.

Axel, Layla and Priscilla rushed after Max and Axel questioned, "How do we protect the stone and stop Scarlett and her friend?"

"The wind element stone is related to Galesia and

can access the many portals and secret passages here.", replied Max.

"So, all we have to do is lure them into a portal?", questioned Layla.

"Yup!", exclaimed Max, smiling.

"Won't they come back after?", asked Priscilla, puzzled.

"That's why we'll use the element stone. When Galesia uses her powers, it can lock out a creature from Galesia for only a few minutes, but this element stone can lock them out permanently!

That way, we won't have to worry about them damaging Galesia!", stated Max, looking around.

After a while of flying, Max spotted the creatures and whispered, "There!"

The four stopped above the creatures, that were creating destruction...

"You see, all the trees open up a portal to different locations. I'll open up the passages when you three lure those creatures towards any of the tree...", added Max.

"Sounds like a plan to me!", said Layla, landing on the ground.

"Hey!", exclaimed Layla, drawing the creatures' attention. "You've probably heard of cat and mouse, so we'll be the mouses and you all be the cats!"

Axel and Priscilla landed beside Layla and transformed into mouses. Layla also transformed into a mouse and squeaked.

The creatures chuckled and divided and rushed after each of them. There were about 6 of them.

Layla stopped in front of a tree and squeaked again. 3 creatures surrounded her and they pounced on her.

Layla quickly jumped and transformed into an eagle. She then rapidly landed and transformed into an elephant.

Max then opened up a passage and Layla then pushed the creatures into the portal.

Axel paused in front of 2 creatures in a way that the creatures back faced a tree. Max opened another passage and Axel transformed into a cheetah and jumped on the creatures to push them into the portal.

Priscilla transformed into a human and stood with her back facing a tree and a creature in front of her.

The creature decided to pounce and ran towards Priscilla. When the creature was very close to the tree, Priscilla jumped over the creature and used its head a support to land on the ground. The creature then fell into the portal and Max closed the portals.

"Yeah!", exclaimed Max, landing.

"That was easy...", stated Priscilla, smiling.

That's when something pushed Max to the ground. It snatched the wind element stone and flew in the air.

Axel looked at the creature and questioned, "An eagle?"

"You forgot me too quickly... Well, after this moment, you'll never forget me!", exclaimed the eagle, grinning.

The Mystery of the Element Stones

"Scarlett?!", questioned the four, in union.

"Yes, and now with this precious stone, I can finally unify it my power!", stated Scarlett, smiling.

That's when the sylph appeared. The sylph took away the air element stone from Scarlett's grip and gave it back to Max.

"Go! I'll deal with her. Find the person who will bond with the stone.", stated the sylph.

Max was not ok with this and exclaimed, "We can't leave you alone with-"

That's when a gush of wind started pushing all of them back.

The four and sylph turned their gaze towards Scarlett.

They then noticed that Scarlett knew a lot of powerful spells. Scarlett smiled and then shot a wind spell.

The wind spell contained a lot of dust and dirt and it whirled around the sylph.

"Sylph are pure air spirits and can't handle pollution! It's one of their weaknesses!", exclaimed Max, panicking.

Max then tried to shoot a powerful wind attack, but Scarlett used the wind element stone to absorb the attack! She then sent the same attack back to the ground!

"Run!", exclaimed Max, running. Priscilla, Layla and Axel jumped off as soon as the wind attack hit to ground!

The wind attack was so powerful that it seemed to have penetrated the ground to a great extent!

"Woah!", exclaimed Priscilla, looking at the huge hole that had been formed.

"That was exciting!", stated Scarlett, chuckling. She then turned to the sylph, who seemed to be injured badly.

"Looks like you'll have to announce me as the holder of the element!", exclaimed Scarlett, smiling.

"Never! The element will find its owner!", exclaimed the sylph, covering her wounds.

Suddenly, Scarlett was hit by a fireball! She was pushed back; however, she used the air element stone to minimize its effect.

"You know, air beats fire!", remarked Scarlett, creating a tornado.

The tornado slowly grew in size, rapidly. Scarlett called out to the sylph, and said, "You know that you can stop all of this by announcing me as the owner of the element stone, right?"

"The element stone is not something to be given, it is something to be earned! Not even I, have the power to give to someone worthy. And even if I could announce the owner, it wouldn't be you!", exclaimed the sylph, tearing open the pollution whirlpool that surrounded her.

"Looks like we're doing this the hard way then...", stated Scarlett.

The sylph smiled and called the element stone back to herself. The element stone quickly teleported from Scarlett's grip to the sylph's light caressing touch.

"No matter how hard you try, the element stone will always be called back to Galesia.", said the sylph.

"I thought that may happened…", stated Scarlett, landing on the ground. "So, I came prepared…"

That's when three more of the dark creatures landed beside Scarlett.

"More?!", questioned Layla, in disbelief.

"Oh, these are not even a few…", replied Scarlett. "Get the stone boys."

The dark creatures turned her heads around and sensed the element stone in the custody of the sylph.

"I'll be going now! I have a nature stone to find!", called out Scarlett, flying away.

The dark creatures started to walk towards the sylph and surrounded her completely. Priscilla *landed in front of the sylph and whispered, "Hold on!"*

She then raised her arm and punched the ground! The ground started to crack and divided the land into several pieces. One of the creatures seemed to have fallen into the crack and landed about a few feet below.

Axel then poured lava into the cracks and the lava devoured the creature that had fallen into the crack previously.

"Let's play 'The floor is lava', shall we?", questioned Axel smiling.

Just then, the creature that had fallen into the crack disappeared.

The other two creatures groaned. Suddenly, something unexpected happened…

Wings broke out from the back of the dark creatures! The crack then spread more towards the creatures; however, the creatures easily solved that problem by flying!

"Looks like you know how to play this game!", exclaimed Layla flying in front of the creatures,

smiling.

"Now let's play another game. Dodge Ball!", exclaimed Axel.

The dark creatures chuckled, however were interrupted when Axel shot a fireball at them!'

One of the creatures failed to dodge the fireball and disappeared.

"You didn't let me finish. What I meant to say was 'Dodge Fireballs!'", stated Axel, smiling and rolling a fireball on his finger.

He then released the fireball at the other creature, with great force!

The fireball hit the creature and vapor evolved all around…

"Too easy!", stated Layla, relieved.

That's when another fireball emerged from the smoke and went right past Layla!

"Or not!", exclaimed Layla.

The smoke revealed the dark creature creating

another fireball!

"They can do that?!", questioned Max, reducing the tornado.

"Apparently, they can.", stated Priscilla, looking at Max. That's when an idea popped up in her head!

"Max! Direct that tornado towards the creature!", exclaimed Priscilla.

"Oh, yeah!", said Max, launching the tornado towards the creature.

However, the creature opened its mouth and the tornado went inside it!

"Did it just… drink the tornado?", questioned Axel, confused.

The dark creature then allowed the strength of the tornado to flow through the fireball and it then launched the fireball towards Priscilla!

Max stepped in and used his powers to change the direction of the wind so that the fireball would go back. And he succeeded in doing so!

The fireball retraced its path and hit the creature!

However, it wasn't strong enough!

The dark creature paused in the air a few feet and looked up.

Layla was shocked and said, "How-"

Axel quickly placed his palm on Layla's mouth before she could say anything else.

Layla became furious and used her telepathy powers and communicated, "Why'd you that?"

Axel used his telepathy powers to connect his thoughts with Layla, Priscilla and Max. Then he stated, "Look at the creature, he's confused about where we are even though the smoke is gone. It almost like…"

"It's blind…", added Priscilla, watching the dark creature struggle.

"And it depends on its ability to hear to find us!", added Max.

"So, how can we be sure that it won't shoot attacks randomly?", questioned Layla.

That's when the creature shot an attack towards

Layla! Layla reversed the attack and shot it back at the creature. The creature seemed to have been injured by this as it held its arm tightly.

"How'd it know where to shoot?", questioned Priscilla.

"Either it shot it randomly, or it heard something…", replied Max.

The creature then shot another towards Axel! Axel dodged it rapidly.

"That wasn't random… It must be having an acute sense of hearing… Maybe its hearing the movement of air?", stated Axel.

"What?", asked Layla, Priscilla and Max, in unison.

"Whenever we move, we displace some air particles, right? So, it must be trying to hear the movement of the air particles. It's like, when we play badminton, we swing the racket and we hear a slight 'whoosh!' sound.", stated Axel.

"How do we defeat this guy without moving or talking then?", asked Priscilla, lost.

"I guess we take the risk of doing both!", exclaimed Axel, speaking aloud to grab the creature's attention.

The creature turned in the direction of Axel's voice, and shot a fireball at him!

Axel smiled and his element stone rose. The element stone then absorbed the power of the fireball and the fireball disappeared. The element stone fell back and Axel chuckled.

"Wrong move, buddy!", exclaimed Axel.

The sylph became happy that the four were able to protect Galesia from the dark creatures. She then let out a sigh of relief.

The creature seemed to have heard the sylph sigh and it shot the fireball at the sylph! The sylph tried to move but noticed that there were remnants of pollution at the feet that trapped her!

The fireball rapidly decreased the distance between itself and the sylph. That's when Max did something unexpected!

Max stepped in and blocked the fireball from hurting the sylph, but… the fireball hit him!

The fireball hit Max hard and pushed him back. Max crashed into several trees and then landed far away, badly wounded.

"Max!", exclaimed Priscilla, tearing up. She then turned to the creature, her eyes flaring up.

Priscilla then grew long thick weeds and exclaimed, "If you mess with my friends, you mess with me!" Saying so, the weeds shot their way to the creature and tied it up tightly. The weeds seemed to tighten their grip as every second passed.

Suddenly, something unexpected happened. The creature absorbed the power of the weeds and the weeds withered and shrunk. Priscilla was taken aback by this.

The creature groaned once again and grew stronger weeds and send them to capture Layla, Axel and Priscilla.

Axel tried to use his element by absorbing the power of fire in the weeds. But the harder he tried to set himself free, the tighter the weeds got…

The sylph, on the other hand, was trying her best to move, and keep the air element safe.

The air element then rose and travelled away from the sylph… It then found Max, and it landed on Max.

The dark creature, on the other hand, was growing in power…

"The weeds are getting tighter…", stated Axel, struggling. He then used his element and burned the weeds that surrounded him. Axel landed on the ground and looked up.

The dark creature looked down and used its arm to punch the ground where Axel stood. Axel did a backflip and landed a little away.

Just then, a tornado arose… It gathered around the creature and engulfed the weeds, destroying them. Layla and Priscilla were taken out of the tornado by the air and the two landed beside Axel.

Priscilla smiled and looked up. She then exclaimed in joy, "Max!"

Max landed on the ground and looked at a scar. He touched it and was shocked to feel no pain.

"Nice!", exclaimed Max, surprised.

Priscilla rushed to Max and hugged him. Axel and Layla smiled and also joined in. Priscilla then stated, "You scared us badly!"

"Sorry…", said Max, smiling.

Axel then looked at the tornado. "The tornado's looking stronger… But it might need some amplification…" Axel then used his element stone to amplify the effect of the tornado!

The tornado grew larger, and the creature soon disappeared! The tornado then burst open into fresh air and fire, that spread through every part of Galesia, and repaired all the damages caused by the dark creatures and Scarlett.

The fresh was followed by a glow that made everything look… beautiful…

"Woah! I've never seen anything so gorgeous before…", stated Layla, looking around, awe-struck.

"And a friend of mine may have told me where we can find the nature element stone…", stated Max, smiling.

"Really? Where?", questioned Priscilla, excitedly.

"The nature element stone is in… drumroll please…", requested Max.

The wind changed its course in such a way that you could hear a mild drumroll.

"Naturia!", exclaimed Max.

"Naturia?", asked Axel, puzzled. "Why would it be there?"

"To be honest, I don't know. Like I told you, a friend told me…", replied Max.

"What's their name?", questioned Axel.

"The pixie who- Oh! Nevermind.", stated Max, realizing that it was Scarlett who was trying to misguide them.

"Just because Scarlett told you that, doesn't mean it's not in Naturia. How can, we be sure?", remarked Priscilla, trifle bewildered.

"I think a friend of mine might know…", stated Axel, smiling.

He snapped his fingers and teleported. However, Layla, Priscilla and Max were still at the plains…

"Hopefully, he will come back with the location of the nature element…", said Layla, sitting on the shining grass that reflected the sunlight.

"Travelling from dimensions to dimensions is really… tiring…", stated Priscilla, falling back on the grass.

"You can say that again…", added Max, floating in the air, relaxing.

"I wonder how many elements exist…", murmured Layla.

"Infinite!", exclaimed Max, his eyes closed.

"Huh?", questioned Layla.

"You asked how many elements exist. There are infinite elements.", repeated Max, calmly.

"Really? I can think of only four. Fire, Air, Earth and Water…", said Layla, thinking deeply, counting her fingers as she named each element.

"What Max means to say is, that there are different KINDS of elements. Fire, Air, Earth and Water are well known since they are all around us, and constitute life.", added Priscilla, looking at the clouds that were floating lazily in the sky.

"Woah... So, what are the other elements?", asked Layla.

"Weather.", replied Priscilla, sitting up. "Weather is another element. But it can be controlled by air element." Priscilla turned to Max as she said this.

"So, air is the primary element, and weather is the secondary which falls under the element air?", questioned Layla.

"Yup! Out of the elements I know, there are two other primary elements, the most powerful ones actually.", replied Max, opening his eye.

"Which are?", questioned Layla, impatiently.

"You want to do the honors, Priscilla?" questioned Max, looking at Priscilla, smiling.

Priscilla nodded and turned to Layla and replied, "Sun and Moon."

"I thought phoenixes were associated with the sun...", stated Layla, confused.

"Correct. But let me emphasize a word there. Phoenixes are ASSOCIATED with the sun. We phoenixes can't perform the most powerful spells related to heat and the sun. Also, the holders of the sun and moon element can control the rising and setting of the sun and moon respectively!", exclaimed Priscilla, smiling.

"Wow! So where are these element stones?", questioned Layla, curiosity twinkling brightly in her sky-blue eyes.

"No one knows.", replied Max, closing his eyes again, sighing.

"Why?", asked Layla. "I mean, some creature or the other knows the location of the fire and air element stones and most probably, also the water and nature element stones."

"That is true, but it was believed that the sun and moon element stones were very powerful. Holders of these elements, if not responsible, can cause chaos and disharmony...", stated Max, sitting up in the air, his eyes wide open.

"I... still don't get it...", said Layla.

"The sun and moon element stones are capable of

possessing powers of other elements as well, like fire, air, water, earth and every other element known to all kind!", exclaimed Priscilla, creating an illusion.

"Max, a little help in explaining?", requested Priscilla.

"No problem!", replied Max, floating over to Priscilla and the illusion she was creating.

"You know that magic existed before animals started to live on Earth, right?", questioned Max.

Layla nodded rapidly.

"Well, before magic came into existence, the element stones were formed… But the sun and moon element stones were the only ones formed…", narrated Max, pointing at two of the illusions shaped like crystals, one yellow and the other blue.

"It is usually said that, the sun element stone let out a powerful aura which bundled together to form the sun, and the aura of the moon element stone bundled to form the moon…", added Priscilla, showing an illusion for it.

"All our dimensions are in another galaxy… Like this one. The first two people to be the holders of these element stones were the two siblings, Andrea and André. They were the first and only loyal holders of the element stones…", continued Max, the illusion being blown away by him.

"What happened?", questioned Layla.

Priscilla then continues, "Andrea and André served as the holders for almost 100 centuries."

"100? You know its 2022, right? That's nowhere close to 10,000 years!", interrupted Layla.

"Time is funny in different dimensions. Especially the B.C. on Earth.", replied Priscilla.

"Oh, right! Carry on!", exclaimed Layla.

"After serving as the holders, Andrea and André decided to renounce the element stones and allow the stones to find their new holders. The next two lineage were two people who lived in the same area, however, never knew each other until they were ten.", added Priscilla, showing an illusion of two kids, with shining necklaces around their necks.

"What year was this?", questioned Layla.

"It was around 1953.", replied Max, touching the illusion, continuously.

"That sounds like a year on Earth.", stated Layla.

"Well, the element stones found their next holders on Earth…", added Priscilla.

"Woah! Earth is full of gifted people!", remarked Layla, smiling.

Priscilla smiled and then changed the illusion. She turned to Max. Max nodded and added, "The names of two holders were never known, but what we do know is that they found their way into the mythical world when they were 19."

Priscilla then changed the illusion and narrated, "After a few months, something terrible happened… The two holders suddenly decided to use their stones for personal gain…

They started to imprison creatures, conquered various kingdoms, one of them being the phoenix kingdom itself. When the sun and moon element stones learnt about what the two holders had done over the 4 months, the sun and moon element *stones rose into the sky, never to be seen again…"*

"What about the two holders?", questioned Layla.

"The sun and moon element stones banished them to an unknown place and sealed the portal to get out of the dimension…", replied Max, settling down on the grass softly.

Priscilla made the illusion disappear and sat quietly.

"How long has it been since the sun and moon element stones left?", asked Layla.

"Well, it was 1953 on earth, and they were in the mythical world for 4 months, which is approximately a week… So, about 69 years now…", replied Priscilla.

The three sat in silence for quite a while.

"And I thought I was getting a hang of magical history…", stated Layla, sighing.

"Magical history is infinite… No one can possibly know it all, except magic itself.", stated Max.

"How do you guys know so much about the

magical history?", questioned Layla.

"I loved history a lot as a kid, and spent most of my time in the history isle of the library back at the palace.", replied Priscilla, smiling.

"I went around in different dimensions borrowing books, and learning different things and creatures, like Katherine Loophole.", replied Max, grinning from ear to ear.

That's when Axel popped out of thin air and smiled.

"I know where it is! But I think we will have to go there with lots of explanation, especially you Layla…", stated Axel, smiling.

"Why?", asked Layla.

"The nature element stone is in the Hunters' Forest, on Earth.", replied Axel, smiling.

"Oh, I have soo much to explain!", exclaimed Layla, frustrated, falling back on the grass.

"Well, at least you get to see Dash!", added Axel, trying to make Layla feel better.

"Yeah… I miss Dash… I am hoping to know Kyra as well…", said Layla.

"Oh, right! The kingfisher!", recalled Max.

"I guess we're going home then!", exclaimed Layla, standing up, trying to think of ways to explain why they keeping going to different 'countries.'

Axel pulls Layla, who was unwilling to go back until she figured out a correct explanation.

Priscilla and Max followed them, chuckling. Max and Priscilla took one last look at Galesia and then turned his gaze to the sylph.

The sylph smiled and disappeared into her air form.

Axel created a portal back to Earth, and the four jumped into the portal…

6 Back at Hunters' Forest

The portal seemed to have opened in the middle of the sky and when the four came out of it, they started to fall down immediately.

"We can't use our powers, everyone will notice!", exclaimed Layla.

"Everyone will also notice FOUR KIDS falling in the sky!!", added Max, ready to use his air powers.

Max used his powers to slow down their fall and asked the wind to flow in an upward direction to lighten their fall.

He was successful in doing so! Layla and Axel landed on the ground softly, while Priscilla used another strategy.

When she was deep in the forest for any human to notice her, she grew a weed from her hand and shot it at the branch of a tree nearby. The weed twirled around the branch and extended towards the bark of the tree and held on the bark tightly.

Thanks to the weeds being stuck tightly, Priscilla stopped falling in the middle of the forest, hanging from the weed.

Max, on the other hand, landed on some creature… When Max was about to hit the ground, a creature swooped in and allowed Max to land on itself.

"Seb!", exclaimed Max, smiling.
Seb smiled and Max got off of Seb.

Layla looked at Seb and smiled. She stood up and walked over to Seb, and patted him between his ears.

Seb seemed to have appreciated this and hugged Layla. Layla hugged him back and turned to Max.

"It must be soo awesome to have a wolf friend, especially one like Seb!", exclaimed Layla, smiling.

Priscilla was very high above the ground and used her powers to look at Layla's home. However, no one was in sight…

Priscilla found this weird and decided to search the rest of town. However, no one, not one person was in town…

"Uh… Guys… I hate to be the one to say that

something's wrong, but… you have to see this…",
stated Priscilla, searching the inside of homes as
well.

Layla, Axel and Max grew confused and Axel
questioned, "What do you mean?"

"There's literally, no one in town…", replied
Priscilla, her eyes shaking with terror.

"Well, maybe they are all at home?", questioned
Layla.

"No, they are not. I checked every single home. No
one.", remarked Priscilla, a shiver running down
her spine.

That's when something struck Layla's mind. She
turned to Axel and asked, "Who told you about the
whereabouts of the nature element stone again?"

"Oh! I went to visit Moon hoping she would know
the location, but she told me that she was unaware
of the location, however, the pixie that lives deep
in the forest might know.

So, I visited that pixie and he told me that its
somewhere here.", replied Axel.

That's when Axel realized the reason why Layla asked the question. Axel sighed and questioned, "You think that the pixie, being notorious, tricked me, don't you?"

"What? No… Why would I think that?", asked Layla, smiling.

Axel gave Layla a stern look and Layla stated, "Yeah, that's what I thought…"

"Actually, that pixie told the truth…", stated Max, getting up, Seb by his side.

"How can you be so sure?", questioned Priscilla, landing on the ground with the help of the weeds.

"Because this place is illusional!", exclaimed Max, smiling.

"What?", asked Layla, Priscilla and Axel in unison.

"Mhmm… Scarlett never left Galesia… She thought that if we managed to find the fire element stone, we could also earn the air element stone. So, she decided to stay and watch over us.

When she saw that I bonded with the air element

stone, she knew we'd head for either the water element stone or nature element stone. When Axel came back, she might have used a hearing spell to listen to the whereabouts of the nature element stone, and might have spiked our portal with a spell to lead us here! An illusional replica of Earth!

She wanted to keep us here for a long time, so, she thought of making it seem like everyone was in danger here. We, being curious, would've definitely started searching…

She was so confident that this would work that she missed a major detail…", narrated Max, stepping down beside Seb, patting him.

"Seb always wears a necklace I gave him when I first met him…", stated Max, smiling at the illusional Seb.

The illusional Seb was clueless that Max had figured out everything and did its role to enact Seb.

"That was a great observation, Max!", exclaimed Axel. "Oh, wait. That means Scarlett's probably looking for the nature element stone on Earth right now."

"Oh, trust me. She has to do a lot of fitting in

before she goes about finding the element stone…", said Layla, creating a portal. "Let's go!"

The four once again jumped into the portal, but this time, into the correct one.

They then landed on the grounds next to the entrance to the Hunters' Forest.

"Well, at least this time we didn't fall…", stated Max.

Layla, Axel and Priscilla looked at Max, a huge question mark on their faces.

"Come on! We landed safely this time! And no one saw us!", exclaimed Max.

"Don't be so sure, Max!", exclaimed a voice.

The four turned back immediately and breathed a sigh of relief.

"Dad! You gave us a jump scare!", exclaimed Layla, laughing.

"Well, Mom told me that you might come. And here you are!", stated James, smiling. "So, which element stone is here?"

The Mystery of the Element Stones

"Element stone? What is that?", questioned Max, confused, trying to hide the fact that they were searching for the element stones.

"You're overdoing it…", whispered Priscilla.

"You thought I wouldn't notice the element stones?", questioned James.

"We didn't expect anyone to notice!", added Axel, chuckling.

"Well, yours and Max's aura is clearly more powerful and Max is wearing a white necklace and you are wearing a red ring each swirling with energy…", explained James.

"I did expect you to find out, but not that quickly!", stated Priscilla, surprised.

"You four don't know me from my magical origin that well.", remarked James.

"True. We just found out. By the way, how long were we long?", questioned Layla.

"9 days, to be precise…", replied James.

"9?!", questioned the four, in unison.

"Time is pretty funny in different dimensions. It's different in every single dimension. Like if you compare the time on Earth to that in the Enchanted Forest, a day here, is an hour in the enchanted forest.", explained James.

"So, the moon and sun element stones have been gone longer than we thought…", whispered Layla, turning to Max and Priscilla.

"The sun and moon element stones…", said James. "They've been gone 10 centuries according to what we see in the millennium castle."

"Wow! That's a long time!", exclaimed Max.

James nodded slightly and then turned away.

"Come on, you need to explain where you're going next Layla!", exclaimed James, walking away and chuckling.

"Dad!", exclaimed Layla, following James, and being followed by Priscilla, Axel and Max who were laughing.

~

The four and James soon reached home and Layla gulped hard.

Axel smiled and walked over to Layla, lowering his voice to a whisper, "Don't worry! Priscilla, Max and I are here to help you if you fumble while explaining…"

"Thank you…", whispered back Layla, her voice sounding relaxed.

James used one of the spare keys and opened the door and called out, "The four are back!"

James then hung the keys onto a holder fixed in the wall to the right of the door.

"Woof!!", barked Dash, dashing his way out of the living room and bumping into Layla.

Layla chuckled and gave Dash a hug and stated, "I missed you too Dash…"

Dash barked once again and Layla set him down on the ground.

"Layla!", exclaimed Amy, walking towards Layla to give her a hug.

The Mystery of the Element Stones

Layla smiled and hugged Amy back.

"So, what's the new mystery you four are out to solve?", questioned Amy.

"It's about the element stones.", replied Priscilla, pointing at Max's necklace and Axel's ring.

"Fire and Air. Suits you two perfectly.", stated Amy, looking at Axel and Max.

"Oh! Don't worry about giving any explanation, I told Mom and Dad that you four decided to visit different countries and would often come by to visit.", said Amy, smiling.

"Really?", questioned Layla, in disbelief. Amy nodded. Layla sighed and stated, "You're a lifesaver, Mom!"

"And I'm guessing you all are here for the nature element stone. Right?", questioned Amy, confident that the answer would be yes.

"Yup! We just thought that we should visit, since it is evening on Earth…", replied Max, looking out a window next to the door.

"It's actually 7:49 pm right now.", stated James.

"You weren't joking when you said time is funny in different dimensions...", murmured Layla.

James shrugged his shoulders and then said, "Well, dinner's going to be served at 9, and you do have an hour to do some finding in Hunters' Forest, presuming that the nature element stone is there."

"I guess we could use a head-start, especially since Scarlett's here already.", added Max.

"Scarlett?", questioned James and Amy, in unison, puzzled.

"We'll tell you about her later...", stated Axel.

The four then looked around the house and teleported into the interiors of Hunters' Forest.

However, something was different this time they teleported. Layla sat on a branch and looked down. Layla was shocked by this and almost lost balance on the branch.

Axel fell flat on the ground, landing beside some mushrooms.

Priscilla fell out of the sky and used her weed spell once again to save herself. On the other hand, Max turned out to fall onto one of Priscilla's weeds, almost making Priscilla fall. Max tore a weed as he was holding onto it, and held onto Priscilla's leg.

Priscilla then strengthened the weeds. She then slowly let the weeds place Max and herself on the ground.

Layla transformed into a squirrel and rushed down the tree, and then transformed back to a human.

Axel got up and looked around at the others.

"What happened?", questioned Layla.

"Maybe the teleportation turned out weird because it's been a while since we used our powers on Earth...", replied Max.

"Or maybe, Scarlett spiked our teleportation powers...", added Axel, sighing.

"That would mean that she's been here already. Think about it. She must've reached here before us and must've known that we would come here, so she cast some of spell to make our magic go crazy!", exclaimed Layla.

"True, and that would also mean that she's not

found the nature element stone yet!", added Priscilla, relief in her eyes.

"So, where could it be?", questioned Max, looking around. "Because looking at this dense forest right now, it gives me a feeling that we will be searching for that stone for a very… long time…"

"Why is this place called Hunters' Forest anyway?", asked Axel, looking around.

"Because no one would usually enter this place because of the dangerous animals that prevail here.", replied Layla, rapidly.

"I didn't even see a rabbit here!", exclaimed Axel, questioning the name of the forest.

That's when they heard the bushes rustle. Suddenly, a bunny jumped out of the bushes and twitched its ears.

"You were saying?", questioned Layla, sitting and patting the bunny.

"Maybe its best if we use a spell to locate the element stone…", stated Max.

"I know a spell. It allows me to communicate to

the trees. I could ask them for help…", added Priscilla.

Axel and Layla looked at each other and smiled and turned to Priscilla, nodding in agreement. Max also nodded vigorously.

Priscilla smiled and placed her palm on a tree, and allowed her energy to pass through the tree, allowing her to communicate with all the trees.

After a while, Priscilla withdrew her palm and stated, "The trees said they'll try to find it. We could come back tomorrow to see if they found it."

"That's a good idea.", said Layla, looking at her watch. "It's 8:15 pm right now. We could stay here for about half an hour."

"I don't mind staying here and looking around. I really want to see some animals.", said Max, using his powers to fly around, searching the bushes.

The four agreed to stay for a while and wandered around the forest. They all enjoy their time at the forest.

Axel and Layla bonded with the bunny and the bunny introduced its family to them, Priscilla decided to grow a few flowers and trees in the forest and used her magic to grow them effortlessly and Max floated in the air lazily, looking at the stars and Moon.

Layla and Axel were talking to the bunny when one of the other bunnies hopped out of the bush, holding a small locket between its teeth. The bunny then hopped towards Layla and Layla held out her hand. The bunny placed the locket lightly on her hand and sat there.

Layla patted the bunny and opened the golden locket. She blew of the soil on the photo inside the locket and stared at the photo, which was a bit wet with the soil.

"Hey, Axel… Does this girl have red hair?", questioned Layla, showing Axel the photo.

Axel studied the blur picture for a while and replied, "Honestly, it is difficult to make out, but now that I look closely, it does seem like this girl has red hair."

"Maybe it belongs to a girl who might have wandered into the forest. The girl does look pretty young. See?", questioned Layla, showing Axel the locket again.

"Oh, yeah. Keep with it you for now, we might find that girl, if she wanders into the forest again.", stated Axel.

Layla nodded and kept the locket in the back pocket of her jeans.

"We could also try and find that boy in the locket. If we do find him, we could tell him that his best friend lost it.", said Axel, patting a bunny lightly.

"How can you be sure that they're best friends? They could be siblings as well…", stated Layla, making a valid point.

"I don't think so. The two look very different the girl has red hair and the boy has black hair.", stated Axel, confidently.

"I guess we'll figure out once we find either of them then…", stated Layla, smiling.

On the other side of the forest, Max was floating lazily in the air, when the air began to talk to him. Max listened carefully and followed the direction of air.

The air led him to behind a few bushes that led him to a floating crystal. Max suddenly felt a strong negative aura being radiated by the crystal that floated… Max used his powers and requested the air, "Please bring Priscilla here."

The air seemed to have accepted Max's request as it pushed Priscilla to where Max was. Priscilla landed beside Max and asked, "Max, what happened? The air just brought me here…"

"It's that crystal… I feel a strong negative aura coming from it…", whispered Max.

"We shouldn't touch it, we might end up absorbing its aura…", added Priscilla.

"Well, we can't leave it here either…", remarked Max. "Someone innocent may end up absorbing its aura as well."

"Can the wind place it somewhere else?", asked Priscilla, worriedly.

Max communicated with the wind and said, "The wind said that the negative aura pollutes it badly, and could also cause some other problems…"

Max thought for a while and then an idea popped in his head. He asked, "Maybe the weeds can grapple around it and quickly place it under the *earth before the weeds wither?"*

"That would end up in the trees absorbing the aura, which is even worse.", remarked Priscilla.

"Then, I guess fire's the only way we can stop this crystal from hurting anyone...", stated Max.

Priscilla nodded slightly, staring at the crystal. Max whispered to the wind, "Ask the bunnies to inform Layla and Axel to come here..."

The wind instantly travelled to the bunnies and whispered a low tune into their ears. A bunny dropped its ears and grabbed Layla's attention.

"Aw... What happened?", asked Layla, looking at the bunny.

The bunny turned its head behind the bushes and looked back at Layla.

"Axel, I think this bunny wants us to follow it...", whispered Layla, in a serious tone.

Axel sensed the danger and nodded. Layla looked back at the bunny and said, "Will you guide us?"

The bunny turned its ears up and hopped away.

Layla and Axel got up and rushed behind the bunny.

Soon, they found themselves staring at a crystal, radiating a powerful negative aura.

"That's a strong aura... I've never come across anything like it before...", whispered Axel, frowning.

"We thought you could use the fire element to burn it...", whispered Max.

Axel was a bit startled when he saw Max and Priscilla by his side all of a sudden, but then calmed down.

"You gave me a scare!", exclaimed Axel, panting. "I could try to use a fire spell"

"But?", questioned Layla.

"The fire could sputter everywhere, and this is a forest... So, it could end up in a forest fire instead...", added Axel. "That's why we need to find another way to stop its aura..."

The four stood in silence as they glanced fearfully at the crystal. That's when Layla remembered something.

Priscilla turned to the others and stated, "Remember the spell we used to extract the negative aura out of Marcelo, we could use that spell. We can extract the aura and then that crystal would turn into a regular stone."

"But we still need to store it in something strong…", remarked Max, remembering the shield they cast around Marcelo to trap the aura.

"What if we put the aura into a dark creature?", asked Axel.

"If you mean to say the creatures that helped Scarlett to capture me so that she could enact me, the ones that almost destroyed the whole of Galesia and hurt Max, then we should definitely not put the aura in it!", exclaimed Layla, rapidly.

"I know it's a risky thing, but it's better than polluting the air that may probably result in forming an acidic gas, or causing the trees to absorb the aura and turn into creatures far worse than the dark creatures, or causing a forest fire.", stated Axel.

"He does make a valid point…", added Max.

Layla scoffed and said, "Do you know the consequences of that? We are on Earth! People here will suffer badly if the dark creature absorbs that aura and those creatures can destroy everything!"

Axel noticed Layla tear up a little. He sighed and said, "I know. But if we push the creature into a portal and then allow it to absorb the aura and seal the portal, then we can teleport to the other dimension and make the aura disappear forever…"

"Or we might end up hurting everyone…", added Layla, sadness in her voice.

Priscilla gave out a deep breath and said, "Layla, life is full of risks. If the dark creatures do end up hurting people, then we have to stick together and use our powers to stop it.

We can easily heal the people later, erase everyone's memory on Earth so that they know nothing about what happened…"

Layla inhaled sharply and said, "I guess we could try… I mean, those dark creatures do need to know that they aren't the only ones powerful!"

The four chuckled and smiled.

"Thank you, Layla, for agreeing to this…", said Axel, in a calm voice.

Layla smiled and nodded. Layla turned her gaze to her watch and her eyes grew wide. She then started to run to reach the exterior of the forest!

Axel, Max and Priscilla looked at each other. Priscilla nodded and Max and Axel ran in the direction in which Layla rushed.

They soon caught up with Layla and Max questioned, gasping in between, "What… happened?"

"We're late! It's 9:32 pm!", exclaimed Layla reaching the outskirts of the forest, now increasing her speed to that of a cheetah.

Axel and Max too increased their speed, trying to catch up. Soon, the three reached Layla's home and paused at the fence to catch their breath.

That's when the door flung open and Amy looked around. Amy spotted the three and her eyes widened with surprise.

"What happened to the three of you? And where's Priscilla", questioned Amy, rushing out.

"We found something, and Priscilla decided to stay back, and we realized we were late so we came running back!", exclaimed Max, rapidly.

"Come on! You need to rest, and have dinner...", stated Amy, leading the three into the house.

The three walked down to the dining room, and sat down in a row. They drank some water and waited for a while.

"Mom and Dad went to bed, so did Grandma Emma and Emmy.", stated Amy, walking past the three.

"So, tell us what you found in the forest...", stated James, sitting down in front of the three.

Amy joined James and smiled.

"Well, we were meaning to tell you about Scarlett...", said Axel.

Amy sensed that Scarlett was not a friend and stated, "Go on..."

"We set off to the Millennium Castle for a while. But then, an unusual storm came up, one whose clouds were shaped like a staff…", said Max.

"Did the staff have a crystal?", questioned James.

Layla, Max and Axel all sighed and nodded in agreement.

"The shape of the clouds has not been like a staff, not since around 1954 on Earth…", stated James, thinking deeply.

"Wait…", said Layla, a thought striking her mind. "Dad, are you sure the last cloud shaped like a staff was seen in 1954?"

"Pretty sure. The staff with a crystal was surprisingly said to have a strong controlling aura. It electrocuted creatures and suddenly the creatures were under the influence of…", said James, thinking hard. "I can't remember their names…"

"Scarlett and Lord Asher…", stated Katherine, appearing from nowhere.

The three turned around in shock, their hearts pounding hard.

"Scarlett?", questioned Max, in disbelief.

"Yes. The two former holders of the sun and moon element stones. Scarlett was entrusted with the moon element stone, while Asher was entrusted with the sun element stone. I believe you know what happened later...", stated Katherine, seating herself beside Amy.

"No wonder Scarlett knows so many powerful spells...", remarked Layla, looking at Axel and Max, recalling the wind spell Scarlett used in Galesia.

"You know Scarlett?", questioned Amy.

"Well, there can be more than one Scarlett.", stated Max.

Axel thought for a few seconds and turned to Katherine. He then asked, "Did Scarlett have, by any chance, red hair?"

"Yes. She was known to have red hair and brown eyes...", replied Katherine.

"Oh, ok...", said Axel leaning back in his chair.

Amy sighed and questioned, "The Scarlett you

know is the Scarlett who was the former holder, isn't she?"

"Yes!", exclaimed Axel, rapidly, resting his hands on the table.

That's when Max heard the wind's call. He heard the message and stated, "Priscilla needs help!"

"Go and help Priscilla. No one will know anything about this.", stated Amy, smiling.

"Thanks Mom!", exclaimed Layla, snapping her fingers.

The three then teleported back to the place where they left Priscilla, and found Priscilla leaning against a tree. Priscilla spotted the three and walked over to them.

"We got your message...", said Layla.

"I was thinking of different spells to shift this crystal, but I couldn't find any. That's when the trees told me that they know where the element stone is...", stated Priscilla.

"Then let's go and find that stone!", exclaimed Layla, smiling.

"What about this crystal?", questioned Priscilla, looking at the crystal, floating in mid-air.

"We have to hold it in a shield… Maybe we can use the Marsium extract to strengthen a shield spell…", stated Axel.

Layla looked at the bottle of extract that hung around her neck, almost full with the black powder of Marsium.

"It did hold back a stronger aura than this one, so it could work…", stated Layla, holding the bottle in her hand.

"Priscilla, Max and I can create the shield and you have to pour the Marsium extract. And just to make sure no one breaks this shield, I'll add a finishing touch I learnt from the Realmium…", stated Axel, raising his palm, suddenly conducting electricity.

Layla nodded and Priscilla, Max and Axel stood around the crystal, closing their eyes. Slowly, a small gush of wind began to blow and Max's element stone necklace started to glow…

The wind then increased its pace and grew warmer,

and Axel's ring started to glow bright red.

Layla then looked down, watching the grass slowly grow around the crystal, thickening. The wind then whirled around the grass, tightening them around the crystal.

Axel then opened his eyes and exclaimed, "Layla, now!"

Layla nodded and quickly transformed into a bird and flew over the shield that was growing steadily, and poured the Marsium extract slowly. After pouring a little bit of the Marsium extract, Layla closed the bottle and landed on the ground, transforming back into a human.

The shield glowed for a while and then revealed the crystal, placed inside it. The shield then merged into the air to blend in.

"Woah, no wonder you were electrocuted without holding the realmium...", whispered Layla.

Axel nodded and then something struck his head. He turned to Layla and questioned, "What do you mean I got electrocuted without holding the Realmium?"

"I am a little too observant. I realized that your finger was a little bit away from the Realmium. You didn't touch it, although it must've felt that way...", replied Layla, confident.

Axel thought for a while and whispered, "Maybe you are bonded to the element electricity..."

"Electricity?", questioned Layla, confused.

"I'll tell you about it tomorrow...", added Axel. Layla nodded and the four turned to return home...

Soon, the four reached Layla's home, had dinner and went to bed.

~

The next morning, Layla was awoken by Dash. Dash pushed Layla's hand with his nose and Layla opened her eyes. When she saw Dash, she sat up on her bed and patted Dash.

Dash then jumped off the bed and stopped next to Layla's desk, with a clock.

Layla looked at the time, and saw that it was 9:07 am. Layla got out of bed and freshened up. She then headed downstairs and walked into the living room. When she saw no one in the living room or the adjoining dining room, she realized she woke up early.

Dash paused beside Layla and gazed at the window.

"It feels like a decade since I've been home like this...", stated Layla, looking outside the window, lost in thought.

"Looks like you're an early bird like me as well...", stated James, walking into the living room, and pausing next to Layla.

"Good morning, Dad.", said Layla, hugging James.

"Good morning to you too hurricane!", exclaimed James, hugging Layla back. "So, how has it been since you found out magic exists?"

Layla picked up Dash and stated, "Pretty... spontaneous..."

James chuckled and said, "Agreed. Magic is really unpredictable. One second, you're a normal kid on Earth, and the next, you're part human and part phoenix!"

"Yeah, about that… I never really understood one thing…", remarked Layla, turning her gaze to James.

"What might that be?", questioned James, confused.

"Why am I part phoenix? I mean, Mom isn't a phoenix, neither are you. Then, how am I one?", asked Layla.

"Well, there might have been someone in my family that was a phoenix…", replied James, recalling that Celia is the only person he has that helps connect him to his real parents.

Layla noticed the sadness in her father's eyes and said, "Maybe your mom and dad are still out there, looking for you and Celia…"

"Maybe…", repeated James, lost in thought. He then smiled and stated, "Anyways, about you being a phoenix, creatures are just born with a few qualities that differ from their family…"

"So, me being a phoenix is one of those qualities?", asked Layla, trying to connect a few dots.

James nodded and said, "I also feel like you might

be bonded to electricity…"

"That's the third time someone said that to me…", stated Layla, recalling her grandma Katherine and Axel telling her the same thing. "But, how can you be sure?"

"Axel told me last night that you weren't electrocuted by the Realmium's protection electric shield…", stated James.

"True…", said Layla, recalling the electric shield the four built around the crystal the previous night.

"So, do you want to help me prepare breakfast?", questioned James, smiling.

"Of course! The chefs are in the house!", exclaimed Layla, setting Dash down, who jumped around enthusiastically.

James chuckled and Layla and James headed to the kitchen to prepare breakfast!

~

Time flew by as James and Layla prepared breakfast! Soon, everyone was at the table having the fruit salad, coffee and pancakes at around 9:20 am.

"These waffles are amazing!", exclaimed Max, taking another bite of his chocolate flavored waffles.

"Well, Layla has learnt from the best…", stated James, smiling at Emma, who smiles at everyone proudly.

Everyone chuckles at this.

"The fruit salad has the perfect combo of fruits as well…", stated Priscilla, eating an apple.

"Coffee rules!", exclaimed Axel, raising his mug of warm coffee.

"Agreed!", added Amy, sipping coffee.

"Layla, you haven't told us where you four went?", questioned grandpa Lucas.

"We went to Rome recently!", stated Priscilla, smiling.

"I clicked a few pictures as well.", said Axel, taking out pictures from his bag.

Axel passed the pictures down to everyone, who admired the beauty of Rome.

"The picture of the Colosseum makes me want to buy tickets to Rome right now!", exclaimed Phoebe, smiling.

"We all can go there sometime. But I am hoping that you four have visited many more places. We get to travel through the cities thanks to these pictures you click!", stated Emmy, looking at another picture.

"The pictures were all taken by Axel. He has a strong passion for photography!", exclaimed Layla, sipping coffee.

Axel smiled warmly and took another bite of the fruit salad.

After a while, everyone had finished breakfast and the four were cleaning up.

"Axel, when did you go to Rome?", questioned Layla, curiously.

"When I was a 14-year-old. This was actually the first picture I ever clicked with my camera!", exclaimed Axel, showing the picture of the

Colosseum.

*"Woah! How many countries have you visited?",
asked Priscilla.*

*"I have only visited five countries. Most of the
other times, I was travelling in either the
Enchanted Forest, or the Naturia. Mainly, I
would spend my time at the Millennium Castle.",
replied Axel, leaning against the kitchen counter.*

"The real one?", questioned Max.

"Huh?", questioned Axel, confused.

*"The real Millennium Castle or the dummy one?",
added Max.*

"The dummy one.", replied Axel.

*"We really need to come up with a name for the
dummy castle…", stated Layla, sitting on a chair.*

*The others agreed. Soon, silence conquered the room
as the four turned their gaze outside the window.
It had been quite a while since the four sat down
and admired the beauty of the world that exists.*

The four were all thinking about the same thing,

how their lives had turned from normal to completely adventurous…

"It's hard to believe that I was once a little girl who knew nothing about magic…", said Layla, sighing.

"It's hard for me to believe that I was once a princess who had no friends to share her opinions with…", added Priscilla, her voice shaking.

"It's hard to believe I was once a phoenix who liked to go on adventures by himself…", added Axel, recalling his young self.

"It's hard to imagine what I would be without you guys as my best friends…", added Max.

"I can't even think what would've happened if we hadn't met each other…", stated Priscilla.

The four glanced at each other and realized that they were indeed the people who had changed each other's lives…

That's when a letter popped out in thin air in front of Priscilla.

Priscilla took the letter, and read it. Her eyes grew

wider and wider as she continued to read the letter.

"What does the letter say?", questioned Layla.

"Scarlett's been to the phoenix dimension. This letter is from one of the physicians stating that her army of dark creatures has captured every phoenix in our dimension…", stated Priscilla.

"What?!", exclaimed Layla, Axel and Max, in unison.

"It also says that they had a leader who asked about our location, but no phoenix has told him anything yet… The realmium has switched its location to protect itself.", added Priscilla, nervously.

"Leader?", questioned Layla, turning to Axel, recalling what Katherine told them.

"Lord Asher…", replied Axel, his voice shaking with fear.

Axel filled Priscilla in about who Lord Asher was and how he and Scarlett were once the holders of the sun and moon element stones.

"We have to find the nature element stone! If we

wait any longer, Lord Asher will conquer another dimension!", exclaimed Priscilla.

"Let's go!", exclaimed Axel, rushing into the living room.

The others followed him to the door, but that's when they ran into someone.

"What happened?", asked Amy, sensing danger.

"Scarlett and Lord Asher have taken over the Phoenix kingdom! We need to find the nature element stone!", stated Layla, rapidly.

"I'll tell everyone you four have set out on another trip! Go!", exclaimed Amy, opening the door, urging the four to go.

"Thanks Mom!", exclaimed Layla, rushing outside, followed by Axel, Priscilla and Max.

The four rushed to the back of the house and teleported to Hunters' Forest. Priscilla communicated with the trees and said, "The nature element stone is in the passage to the Hunters' Forest..."

"Of course!", exclaimed Layla, recalling the

inscriptions she saw when she went through the passage. "There are inscriptions on the walls, the element stone must be embedded in one of them! I remember seeing something green that glowed… The dead end opens up to the Enchanted Forest and seals becoming soil and grass! That's a sign that the nature element stone controls the passage!"

"Right! Which tree was it again?", questioned Max, looking around.

"My new friend found it…", replied Layla, looking at the bunny that sat in front of a tree, twitching its nose.

Layla rested her palm on the tree bark and the tree revealed once again, the Staircase of Doom.

The four quickly descended the stairs and paused as the cold water came into view.

"I forgot about the water…", stated Layla, shivering.

"How cold could the water possibly be?", questioned Max, stepping into the water.

Once he put a foot on the water, he immediately

jumped back out.

"Okay. That cold!", exclaimed Max, shivering.

Axel let out a deep breath and walked down the passage, shivering with every step he took. He paused and looked back.

"Let's go find this element stone guys!", stated Axel, smiling.

"One more thing!", exclaimed Layla. "There's always an illusion. It shows you something you fear the most…"

The four looked at each other and then Priscilla and Max also stepped down the passage.

"There's no illusion we can't fight back!", stated Max, smiling.

Layla smiled and stepped into the water. The four walked down the passage for a while.

After a few minutes, Axel paused and looked at the walls.

"Are these the inscriptions you were talking about?", questioned Axel, running his fingers on a *few letters.*

"Yes! The element stone has got to be here somewhere...", replied Layla, looking at the inscriptions.

Max and Priscilla joined the search. However, Axel was analyzing the text.

"Hey, Layla...", said Axel.

"Hmm?", questioned Layla.

"These texts say that the nature element stone was taken away from the Enchanted Forest a long time back. Some creatures caught hold of it, but a fairy managed to hide it here. Do you think those creatures were Scarlett and Asher?", asked Axel.

"Maybe... Scarlett was pretty powerful back in Galesia. So, it is possible that they caught hold of it once...", replied Layla.

"Oh, I did again...", echoed a familiar voice.

"Guys, duck!", exclaimed Priscilla, ducking down.

Max, Axel and Layla immediately followed and noticed thorns shooting like arrows. When the shower of thorns stopped, Priscilla looked around and spotted a figure smiling in the dark.

"Scarlett…", uttered Priscilla.

"Seems like this element stone is mine!", exclaimed Scarlett, smiling, the nature element stone floating in her hand. "How about we invite my friends?"

Suddenly, the pieces of soil and rocks started to collapse from the roof of the passage. At the same time, weeds started to fly out from the ground and dashed towards the four, locking them against the soil.

"You're destroying the passage!", exclaimed Priscilla, trying to pull against the weeds.

"You know the weeds will get tighter the more you pull…", stated Scarlett, smiling.

Priscilla then realized something. Her hands glowed green and she stopped pulling against the weeds. Soon, the weeds around her loosened and were ready to shoot at anyone!

"Thanks for the tip!", exclaimed Priscilla, shooting the weeds towards Scarlett, pushing her against a wall.

The nature element stone floated in its place. Priscilla carefully grew the weeds around the stone and hardened the weeds around it.

She then set Layla, Axel and Max free from the weeds, and used the same weeds to stabilize the roof.

Layla, Axel and Max smiled and used their power to help Priscilla.

"We'll take care of the roof. Go and make sure Scarlett doesn't get to the stone again!", stated Layla.

Priscilla nodded and stepped between Scarlett and the weeds protecting the stone.

Scarlett burned the weeds easily and smiled at Priscilla.

"Getting that element stone will be a piece of cake…", stated Scarlett, fire burning in her hands.

"Don't be so sure!", exclaimed Priscilla, shooting weeds and thorns at Scarlett.

Scarlett built an air shield around her and managed to return a few thorns back at Priscilla!

Priscilla stopped the thorns and looked at the roof of the passage. That's when an idea clicked in her head.

That's when Layla, Axel and Max stopped holding the roof stable and paused beside Priscilla.

The roof trembled loudly this time and began to collapse! Boulders began to fall and swiftly blocked Scarlett's path!

When Scarlett was completely blocked, the four once again stabilized the roof.

"Who knew boulders could stop Scarlett? It was almost too easy!", remarked Max, confused.

That's when light started to glow from the boulders… The boulders then shattered into tiny pieces and revealed Scarlett, who seemed to have casted… a Sun spell!

"A sun spell? No one can cast those, unless…", stated Max.

"Remnants of my element stone are still with me…", concluded Scarlett. "It's sad that I have only one more sun spell left to cast, from what was left behind by my element stone…"

"Then why don't you use that now?", questioned Layla, ready to attack.

"Oh, because there are other powerful spells I know!", replied Scarlett, the dark creatures landing beside her.

The four looked at the roof above Scarlett and saw that the dark creatures had pierced through it.

The four dark creatures caught hold of the four, while Scarlett destroyed the weed protection shield.

"No!", exclaimed the four, in unison, as they saw the nature element stone float in mid-air, no shield surrounding it.

"Thank you… For leading me to this element stone, and upgrading the powers of my friends here with that present you left…", stated Scarlett.

"The crystal!", exclaimed Max, realizing that the crystal had given its aura to the dark creatures.

Priscilla thought for a while and then something struck her mind. Priscilla focused on her powers and suddenly, her powers started to drain out of her!

Her powers flowed into the nature element stone, and the stone glowed brighter…

After a while, Priscilla fell down, weak.

"Your powers are truly great, princess. The nature element stone is even more powerful!", exclaimed Scarlett, kneeling down to look at Priscilla.

Priscilla looked up with a lot of effort and said, "You can never force nature to go against her will. Especially when you are going to use her powers in a bad way…"

Scarlett looked confused.

While Scarlett was talking to Priscilla, Max used his powers to push the creatures back and Axel used his powers to create a fire cage around them. Layla, on the other hand, had poured a few grains of the Marsium extract on the cage to strengthen it against the upgraded powers of the dark creatures!

Scarlett looked up and noticed what had happened.

That's when grass started to grow around the dark creatures and Scarlett.

Scarlett transformed into her eagle form and set

off, taking the element stone with her. But the nature element stone had drifted away from Scarlett and reached the passage again.

Scarlett had disappeared through a portal, not knowing that she lost hold of the element stone.

The element stone grew brighter as the grass drained away the powers of dark creatures. The dark creatures groaned as they slowly became weak.

"How is the element stone not getting affected by the aura of that crystal?", asked Layla, watching the grass pull the dark creatures into the walls.

"Priscilla gave her powers to the nature element stone. Her healing powers protected it from the negative aura.", replied Max, helping Priscilla up.

The grass had now left no sign of the dark creatures, except a glowing black rock…

Layla picked up the black rock and asked, "Looks like an essence…"

"Hey guys… There's something changing on this wall…", stated Priscilla, looking at the wall that was being carved on its own.

Layla, Axel and Max turned their gaze to the inscriptions glowing as they carved the wall of the passage.

Max noticed that there were about 4 figures on one side and 5 on the other, and a text still being written. He read it out loud, "The nature element stone found its holder here… The holder had proved herself…"

"What?", questioned Priscilla, confused. "It hasn't found its holder yet…"

"Maybe it has…", stated Layla, smiling.

"What do you mean?", asked Priscilla, a little weak without her powers.

Max pointed at the nature element stone that floated behind Priscilla. Priscilla turned her gaze to the stone. She was shocked to see it float towards her!

She gently held the nature element stone on her palm. The nature element stone glowed and then allowed Priscilla's powers to flow back through her.

After Priscilla regained her powers, the nature

element stone shapeshifted to a bracelet, with green jewels embedded in it.

"You're the holder of the nature element stone.", stated Max, smiling.

Layla and Axel nodded and grinned from ear to ear.

Priscilla looked at the bracelet and then at her friends. She smiled warmly.

"Now, let's fix this place up.", stated Priscilla, using her new powers to reassemble the pieces of earth that had fallen.

Soon, the roof of the passage was good as new! Max used his element stone to help hold the roof up and give it strength. Axel used his element stone to give the water in the passage a bit of warmth and spread warmth through the passage as well.

Layla used a water spell she knew and drained it into the soil for the trees.

"There's one thing I didn't understand...", remarked Max.

"What?", questioned Axel.

"*Layla mentioned that there would be an illusion. But there wasn't one…*", replied Max.

"*This passage tries to send anyone who enters here away for as to protect the Enchanted Forest.*", added Priscilla. "*Once it realizes that a creature means no harm, it doesn't cast an illusion.*"

"*Guys… The inscription is changing again…*", said Layla, looking at the wall closely. "*It's written in Italian.*"

"*What does it say?*", asked Axel, eagerly.

Layla read the inscription out loud,

"*L'elemento acqua è collegato alle stelle. C'è di più per l'occhio di ciò che si vede, non lasciarti ingannare da ciò che leggi.*"

Layla then concluded, "*It's written in Italian. It roughly translates to*
'*The element of water is connected to the stars. There's more to the eye than what you see, don't be fooled by what you read*'.*"

"*Connected to the stars?*", questioned Axel, cluelessly.

"It does say 'don't be fooled by what you read'. So maybe there's someone who is connected to the stars…", guessed Priscilla.

"Maybe Moon might know where the water element stone is. Moon and stars are connected, right?", asked Max.

"Star! Remember? Star, the princess of the mermaids. She might know where the water element stone is!", exclaimed Layla, recalling Star.

"Of course! Mermaids live in the infinite ocean!", added Max.

"Oh… So that's what the mermaid realm is called…", said Layla.

"Then let's go!", exclaimed Priscilla, smiling.

"Just a sec.", said Layla, taking her phone out. She shot a few texts to Amy about them leaving.

Layla then smiled and kept her phone in her back pocket and said, "Mom said she'll cover for us."

"Great! Let's go!", exclaimed Max.

Axel created a portal and the four jumped into it.

The Mystery of the Element Stones

Now the four were going to find the fourth element stone, the water element stone...

7 The Infinite Ocean

The four popped into thin air and started to descend towards the water.

"Hold your breath!", exclaimed Axel.

The four held onto their breath just as they fell into the water. They fell back into the water for a while and they began to swim in their human form.

Layla casted a spell that enabled each of them to breathe underwater.

"Where did you learn this spell?", asked Axel, fascinated by the effect of the spell. "Usually, these kinds of spells are difficult to cast…"

"The phoenix castle library. It had a book full of different spells. I learnt it from there.", replied Layla, doing loops in the water.

"Layla? Priscilla? Max?", questioned a very familiar voice, swimming from the bottom of the ocean.

"Star!", exclaimed Layla, Priscilla and Max, in unison, joyfully swimming towards Star.

The Mystery of the Element Stones

"Hi! What are you guys doing here?", questioned Star, curiosity twinkling brightly in her eyes.

"We were hoping that you might know where the water element stone is.", stated Axel, swimming next to Max.

"The water element stone? Well, you're in the right place! I bet Mom and Dad know something about it!", exclaimed Star, swimming downwards. "Let's go!"

The four smiled at each other and followed Star to the mermaid kingdom.

Soon, the four and Star reached the majestic kingdom of the mermaids. As they swam past the gates, two dolphins greeted them happily!

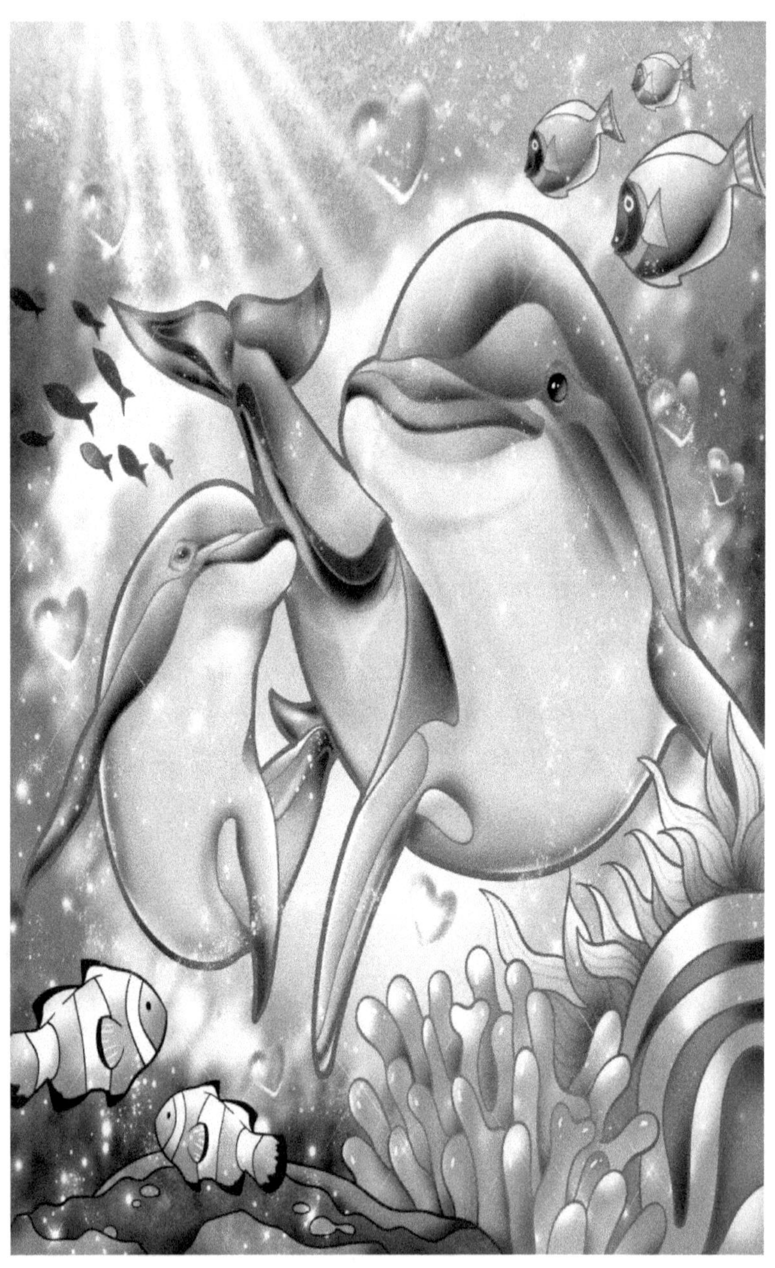

"Hello!", said Layla, watching the dolphins swirl around them.

The dolphin communicated with Layla and Layla smiled and replied, "Of course!"

"What did they say?", asked Priscilla.

"She was asking if we could stop by and play with her for a while. I am sure we can find the time.", replied Layla, grinning from ear to ear.

"Star! Where have you been?", questioned Queen Donna, swimming over to Star.

"Mom! Look who's here!", exclaimed Star, actively swimming behind the four.

"Wait! Who are you?", questioned Star, looking at Axel.

"That's Axel.", replied King Sean.

"You know him?", questioned Layla, Star, Priscilla and Max, surprised.

"Of course! His parents and we are good friends.", replied Queen Donna, smiling.

"It's good to see you again, Aunt Donna and Uncle Sean.", stated Axel.

"Likewise.", reciprocated Donna and Sean, in unison.

"We were hoping you'd know the location of the water element stone…", said Axel, in a serious tone.

Donna and Sean's eye grew small with fear.

"The water element stone was taken away from this kingdom a long time back, by two creatures, greedy for power…", replied Sean, in a low voice.

"What happened to the water element stone?", questioned Layla, worriedly.

"It was taken away by the ocean to the Dark-clawed Scar, the deepest darkest part of the ocean. No mermaid has ever gone there, because of the different spells cast there…", replied Donna.

"Who casted those spells there?", questioned Max, curiously.

"Someone by the name Carla Books…", replied Donna.

"What made her cast spells there?", questioned Axel.

"She just happened to pass by and cast the spells there.", replied Sean.

"If you're going to the Dark-clawed Scar, you must be careful. That place has a way of protecting whatever is placed there.", added Donna.

"It is said that Carla Books may have casted spells there since she wanted to place something valuable there. But, no one knew what that may have been.", stated Sean.

"Who took the water element stone to the Dark-clawed Scar?", asked Max.

"The former queen of Aquira.", replied Donna.

"Aquira?", questioned Priscilla.

"Our kingdom. It is called Aquira. The queen managed to take the water element stone to the Dark-clawed Scar and cast a spell that prevented any creature, including Carla Books herself or any powerful being, from entering the Dark-clawed Scar.", replied Sean.

"Do you know what Carla Books kept in the Dark-clawed Scar?", asked Star, curiously.

"No... Carla Books was the only one who knew.", replied Donna.

"We better head to the Dark-clawed Scar. Scarlett must be headed here.", stated Layla.

"Scarlett?", questioned Donna, Star and Sean, unison.

"You can say that she wants the water element stone, and not for a good cause!", stated Max.

"Can you please give us directions to the Dark-clawed Scar?", questioned Priscilla.

Donna closed her eyes and a piece of paper appeared in her hand. She handed the paper to Priscilla and said, "If you tell this map where you want to go, it will give you the fastest route there."

Priscilla looked at the map and said, "The Dark-clawed Scar."

The map, which was previously showing an image of Aquira, zoomed out of the image of Aquira, and then changed to show a route from Aquira to the what seemed like the Dark-clawed Scar.

"Be safe. The Dark-clawed Scar doesn't welcome visitors very warmly.", warned Donna.

"Thank you for your help, Queen Donna, Star and King Sean.", said Max, smiling.

"Please call us Donna and Sean.", stated Sean.

Max nodded and the four waved goodbye as they headed out of the gates of Aquira to the Dark-clawed Scar…

8 The Dark-clawed Scar

The four followed a route that consisted of several coral, sea horses and various other marine life.

The corals glowed as the sunlight fell on them, the sea horses swam elegantly through the water and the fish giggled as they played.

The dolphins backflipped and played amongst themselves with great joy.

As the four got closer to the Dark-clawed Scar, no creature was in sight...

"They didn't exaggerate when they named this place 'The Dark-clawed Scar'. The name brings out the feeling you get when you slowly enter this place...", stated Max, looking around.

Suddenly, Layla was pushed back!

The four looked around and that's when Priscilla noticed something.

She swam to the place where Layla was pushed back and gave the place a slight push with her palm.

An invisible barrier reflected the light of the sun and revealed itself, before blending in with the water.

Layla moved towards a board near the barrier and read it out loud, "Las heridas sanan, quedan cicatrices. Esta cicatriz se ha quedado mucho tiempo, para mantener algo a salvo."

"What does that mean?", questioned Axel, sure that Layla knew the language.

"It's written in Spanish. It says,

'Wounds heal, Scars remain. This Scar has stayed for a long time, to keep something safe...'", replied Layla.

"This Scar has stayed here pretty long!", exclaimed Max.

Layla, Priscilla and Axel turned to Max and gave him a look.

"What? It has!", remarked Max, truthfully.

The others chuckled.

"Anyways!", exclaimed Max. "How do we get in

there? The former queen of Aquira must've casted a really powerful spell. Sean did mention it can prevent even Carla Books. Wait! Allow me to emphasize. It can prevent even '**The Carla Books**'!"

"True… If Carla Books herself can't get in there again, how will we?", questioned Axel.

"Well, we do have something that she didn't. You know, she didn't have any element stones, and we have three holders here…", stated Layla, smiling.

"The fire element stone could help burn down the barrier…", said Axel, agreeing with Layla.

"Won't the water dowse the fire though?", questioned Priscilla.

"I don't think so. If that we the case, I'd feel a lot weaker. Plus, the fire element stone can find its way through the water.", replied Axel.

"I could make a whirlpool using my element stone…", stated Max, thinking deeply.

"Maybe you can create a small whirlpool in there to break the barrier from inside?", questioned Layla.

"Yeah! That would work!", exclaimed Max, ready to create a whirlpool.

"I could get help from the marine plants to push the barrier to weaken its strength a bit.", added Priscilla, observing the plants.

"I could try to use electricity to weaken the barrier.", stated Layla.

"Great! Sounds like a plan!", exclaimed Max, swirling.

Soon, the four lined up in front of the barrier. Layla, Axel and Max nodded at Priscilla, and Priscilla nodded back.

She then closed her eyes. Slowly, yet steadily, the plants on the other side of the barrier started to grow.

After growing a considerable amount of the length, then shot at the barrier, making the barrier visible, as well as cracks.

Max smiled and extended his arms in front of him. Suddenly, there was rumble…

The air changed its course furiously and started to

form a whirlpool.

Layla then closed her eyes and conducted electricity from her surroundings. Once she created a sufficient amount of electricity, she shot it at the barrier, leaving several glass-like cracks.

"Get ready to merge fire with the electricity...", said Layla, turning to Axel.

Axel nodded and concentrated on his element stone. His element stone glowed bright red, and fire was released by it.

Axel then merged the fire with the electricity quickly and the barrier began to crack more.

Layla then shot a bit of electricity upwards! The electricity rose above the water surface and came down with the same speed and entered the whirlpool!

All the elements combined, fire, electricity, air and nature, broke the barrier!

The barrier shattered and a small push was felt when it happened.

The four looked at each other, smiling.

The Mystery of the Element Stones

"Let's go find that element stone!", exclaimed
Layla, swimming into the Dark-clawed Scar.

Priscilla, Max and Axel followed Layla as well.
After a while of swimming, they came at a fork in
the path.

"Donna was right about the surprises the Dark-
clawed Scar had. This fork in our path, being one
of them.", stated Max.

"We should all spilt up. Maybe each path leads to
something. Remember, Sean and Donna mentioned
that Carla Books placed something valuable here,
that's why she casted the spells in the first place.",
remarked Axel.

"Priscilla and I can take the left path.", stated
Max, pointing to the left.

"We'll take the right one then.", said Layla.

"Remember guys, we broke the barrier, so Scarlett
can come here easily. So, we have to stay alert.",
stated Priscilla.

The other nodded and the four spilt up.

Priscilla and Max headed left and swam over

pointed rocks.

"Hey, I wanted to ask you something…", said Max.

"I am all ears. Shoot!", said Priscilla.

"Why did you give your ruby necklace to the electrum dragon?", asked Max, sadness in his voice.

Priscilla paused in her spot and took a deep breath.

"That was the only way the electrum dragon would've told me the location of the air element stone.", answered Priscilla, in a low voice.

"But, still. You told me your grandmother gave it to you, and that you wouldn't give it to anyone.", added Max.

"My grandmother would've been okay with me giving the necklace for helping all the kingdoms and protecting an element stone from a creature who intends to rule over all the dimensions…", said Priscilla, turning her gaze to Max. "Life is full of challenges, Max. There have been many times in my life I had to choose between two things that were both important."

"Life may throw challenges at us, but it gives us more than the choices we see. There is always another choice which is better than the one we see. We just have to search for it…", remarked Max.

Priscilla eyes grew small with realization and she then smiled.

"That is very true…", stated Priscilla, holding onto her ruby necklace.

Max smiled and started to swim, Priscilla by his side. He then said, "Well, turns out I am finally the one who cheered you up! You've helped me- Ah!!!!!!!!!!!!!!!!!!!!!!!"

Max was cut off when he ran a spiderweb. Priscilla burst into laughter and removed the spiderweb from Max's arm.

"It's just a spiderweb, Max! There's no need to be scared!", exclaimed Priscilla, giggling.

Max said, "I knew that! I just…" Max looked around for a while and continued, "Wanted to cheer you up more! The ruby necklace means a lot to-"

This time, Max stopped talking as he saw a glow

coming from the other end of the cave. He looked at Priscilla, and Priscilla nodded.

The two headed towards the light. After swimming for a while, they paused as they looked at the element stone that floated.

"The water element stone…", uttered Priscilla, mesmerized by its beauty.

"It was almost too easy to find this. I mean, the queen of Aquira must've known someone would come here, so why didn't she leave anything here to protect the stone?", questioned Max, skeptical.

Priscilla seemed to have agreed and looked around. She searched the cave thoroughly, but in vain.

"Maybe Carla Books casted a spell that prevented other creatures from casting a spell in these rooms.", stated Priscilla.

"True. She would've been the only one who can cast protection spells, so any creature who came here wouldn't be able to protect themselves from whatever spell she cast.", added Max, getting an idea of Carla Books might've have done. "That's why there was a fork in the path! This place created a new room for every magical item that is brought here!"

"Just like how a scar leaves a reminder of what happened! These forks in the path are the scars!", exclaimed Priscilla, in recognition.

"Exactly! That means the path Layla and Axel took must have all the spells Carla Books previously casted…", stated Max.

"We should be able to catch up with them if we hurry.", said Priscilla.

Max nodded and grabbed the water element stone. The two exited the small cave and entered the passage.

Suddenly, the room started to rumble.

"We have to swim quicker!", exclaimed Max, taking Priscilla's hand and swimming hard, dodging all the boulders falling.

"Why is the roof collapsing?", questioned Priscilla, following Max.

"Think about it like this. A scar remains only if the event that caused it occurs. The water element stone is that event. Since we took it out of the cave, we technically stopped the 'event' causing the scar to remain. And if there was no event to cause a scar…", stated Max, waiting for Priscilla to complete his sentence.

"The scar never remained!", exclaimed Priscilla.

The two exited the fork just as the boulder blocked the path completely. The boulders then blended together and formed a plain wall, leaving no sign of a room being there.

"There's goes that scar…", said Max.

"We need to go and find Layla and Axel. Before the same thing happens to them.", said Priscilla, rapidly.

Max nodded, but suddenly, something caught his eye. Max swam over to the ground.

"This mermaid scale is not a normal one. Donna and Sean mentioned that no mermaid even comes here.", said Priscilla, swimming next to Max.

"That would only mean that…", said Max, realizing something, terrified.

"Scarlett's gone down this path!", concluded

Priscilla.

That's when something else caught her eye. She moved to where there was previously a left fork in the path and picked something up.

"An essence, of a dark creature...", said Priscilla, showing Max the essence.

Max added, "That means the dark creatures came down our path but got..." Max turned to the wall and continued, "crushed under the boulders, apparently..."

"On the bright side, we don't have to fight off any dark creatures, and, Scarlett is alone down that path.", added Priscilla, looking at the only 'scar' that remained.

"Let's go!", exclaimed Max, swimming down the 'scar'.

"Wait! This path contains the spells Carla Books casted. We have to be prepared to use all the spells we know.", remarked Priscilla, cautiously.

Max nodded firmly and the two headed down the path.

After a while of swimming, they spotted Scarlett. Scarlett had just entered the cave before Max and Priscilla.

Max and Priscilla decided to stay quiet and Priscilla tried to use her telepathy powers to reach Layla.

Luckily, Carla Books hadn't casted a spell to stop telepathy powers, and Priscilla was able to tell Layla about everything.

On the other hand, Layla told Axel about everything, also that Scarlett had followed them.

Layla and Axel then turned to look at the element stone in front of them. They soon realized that it wasn't the water element stone, but it was the electricity element stone...

"The electricity element stone...", said Scarlett, smiling.

Layla and Axel turned around to spot Scarlett right behind them!

"Thank you for leading me to this element stone. That barrier would've been very difficult to break, if it weren't for you four...", stated Scarlett, using *her powers to push Layla and Axel against a wall.*

Scarlett made her way to the electricity element stone, and was about to pick it up.

That's when Scarlett was pushed back by a strong water current. She turned her gaze to its origin and spotted Max and Priscilla!

Max had used his air element stone to throw a strong water current in Scarlett's direction.

"Looks like your friends informed you about that. No wonder I wasn't able to communicate with my friends.", stated Scarlett.

Priscilla quickly used a spell to free Layla and Axel from the wall and the four reunited on one side on the cave, while Scarlett occupied the other.

Scarlett reached out and grabbed the electricity element stone. Suddenly, the cave started to rumble.

"We need to get out of here!", exclaimed Max, guiding everyone out.

Layla noticed that Scarlett had left the electricity element stone in the cave and rushed out immediately.

"We need to leave the element stone!", exclaimed Priscilla.

Layla paused for a while and then the four headed out of the cave as quickly as they could.

However, the cave was collapsing very fast…

While swimming, a boulder fell down on Axel's leg and caught hold of him! Axel tried to pull his leg out, but in vain…

Layla used her powers and broke the boulder using electricity. She and Max caught hold of Axel headed out of the cave.

Layla managed to exit the cave just as a boulder blocked the exit. However, Max and Axel were caught inside the cave…

"Max! Axel! Are you guys, ok?", questioned Layla, worriedly.

"We are okay. Looks like this one scar will always remain, but it's blocked our way out.", replied Axel.

Priscilla spotted Scarlett just as their mermaid tail disappeared into a portal.

"Looks like Scarlett thought the water element stone is somewhere else...", stated Priscilla.

"You have the water element stone, right Priscilla?", questioned Max.

Priscilla took the water element stone out of her pocket and replied, "Yes."

"How will we get you out of there?", asked Layla.

"You guys might have to leave without us...", answered Axel.

"What?!", questioned Layla and Priscilla, in shock.

"Scarlett might be trying to get hold of the sun and moon element stones. If she gets hold of those elements, no one will be able to stop them.", stated Max.

"We're not leaving you here. Priscilla, can you try to move these boulders with the weeds?", asked Layla, hopeful.

Priscilla checked the weeds and concluded, "They've been weakened. When we used them for breaking the barrier, they became weak... The weeds will take a long time to recover."

"These rocks are different as well. They will be difficult to break...", said Axel, examining the rocks from inside the cave.

That's when Layla recalled a spell that involved air, fire, water and electricity.

"I might know a spell. I read it in a book. It was called the Kiarian spell.", stated Layla.

"That spell is way too powerful! It could cause us to lose our powers, permanently.", exclaimed Priscilla.

Layla thought about it and said, "Well, only one of us will be losing her powers then..."

Layla smiled and concentrated on using the fire to heat up the rocks, and used the water to push the boulders from inside.

The water current was now stronger.

"Layla, don't use the spell!", exclaimed Priscilla,

holding onto a nearby rock for support, as the water current was blowing fast.

Layla then conducted electricity and got ready to use all her powers. She merged the water and electricity and created a huge whirlpool.

She then pushed the whirlpool into the boulders! There was a huge splash of water and flash of light…

The light faded to reveal an open exit! Axel and Max got out of the cave and smiled.

Layla, on the other hand, was able to hold onto a few of her powers, but was weak.

Priscilla, Max and Axel noticed Layla's weak state and rushed over to help her.

"See, it wasn't difficult. Plus, I still have a few of my powers…", stated Layla.

Axel noticed something different about Layla and smiled.

He then said, "You have all your powers. The spell just exhausted you."

The Mystery of the Element Stones

Axel then pointed at the necklace Layla was wearing.

Layla looked at it and noticed a wave like shape at the center of the necklace, embedded with a sapphire-like jewel.

"The water element stone gave you the power to cast that spell without losing your powers...", added Max, smiling.

"Also, the electricity element stone.", added Priscilla, grinning from ear to ear, pointing at the small grey crystals attached to the rest of the necklace.

"I thought the electricity element stone was... destroyed by the boulders...", said Layla, confused.

"Well, it is said that the element stones find their way to their holders...", remarked Axel.

Layla glanced at her necklace and something struck her mind.

"Why don't we use the element stones to help this place?", questioned, Layla, rising to swim in front of the Dark-clawed Scar.

The Mystery of the Element Stones

The others smiled and nodded in agreement.

Layla used her water element stone to lift the boulders and clear the path to the cave.

Priscilla used her nature element stone to grow more marine plants around, like corals!

Max used his air element stone to calm the water current and cooled down the water.

Axel used his fire element stone to spread warmth in the ground.

After a while, the Dark-clawed Scar had a completely new look!

It was full of marine plants and animals, warmth, calm waters and a cave that remained as a memory instead of a Scar!

Soon, the mermaids reached the Dark-clawed Scar and looked around in awe.

"This is beautiful!", exclaimed Star, swimming around actively.

"Hey guys! Look at the map!", called out Axel, looking at the map that Donna and Sean had given *them.*

The map changed an image into what looked like the new Dark-clawed Scar and renamed the place as...

"The Caressing Memories...", narrated the four out loud.

"The Caressing Memories, we could leave very valuable items here...", stated Donna, looking at Sean.

Sean nodded and Donna and he turned to the four.

"Thank you, for reviving the beauty of this part of the infinite ocean.", said Sean.

"It was our pleasure...", stated the four, in unison.

That's when something caught Max's eye.

"Guys! Look, the text is changing...", said Max, looking at the board near the entrance of the Caressing Memories.

"You have bonded with your element stones. Now you must stop Scarlett. She resides in a dimension

where she and Asher were banished.

The door was opened not long ago. Since then, they decided to find all the element stones, mainly, the sun and moon element stones.

Scarlett has gone to a dimension where a blue reindeer resides. You may find her create a portal back to the dimension where Asher is…", narrated Axel.

9 Follow that Blue Reindeer!

"Blue Reindeer?", questioned Layla, trifle-bewildered.

"That's very useful!", exclaimed Max.

"Really? You know where a blue reindeer is?", asked Priscilla.

"No! It's not very useful! There will be thousands of dimensions with a blue reindeer! Which one will we go to?!", exclaimed Max, frustrated.

"A blue reindeer?", questioned Star, curiously. "They're found in only one dimension..."

"Oh! I guess I spoke too soon...", stated Max, calming down, surprised.

"Which dimension?", asked Layla.

"The blue reindeers are called Theas, since it is said that the first blue reindeer found was named Thea. They are found in the forest of Maniga.", replied Star, doing water backflips.

"Maniga? I thought that place was only accessed by... Oh... never mind...", said Axel.

"Was only accessed by?", questioned Layla, curiously.

"People related to nature. Obviously, Scarlett must've somehow broken into Maniga, but we can go there easily.", replied Axel, turning to Priscilla.

Priscilla nodded and created a portal to Maniga. The four waved bye to the mermaids and jumped into the portal...

~

The four now landed now ground, surrounded by several trees of incredible height!

"Look! A Thea!", exclaimed Max, pointing at a blue reindeer, standing next to a tree.

The others turned their gaze towards the Thea and then looked around vigorously to spot Scarlett.

"The text told us to find the Thea, but Scarlett's not here…", said Priscilla.

"The text didn't tell us about anything to do after finding the reindeer. Maybe we should follow it. These trees could hold the passage to the dimension where Scarlett was banished.", stated Axel.

"Just like the passage to the Enchanted Forest!", added Layla.

Max turned his gaze to the Thea and saw that the Thea was staring at them…

"Guys, I don't think the Thea trusts us…", whispered Max.

Layla looked confused and walked over to the Thea. The Thea took a step back, cautious.

Layla stepped towards it slowly and assured the Thea that she meant no harm by keeping her arms in the air.

The Thea stared at Layla for a while and then walked towards Layla. Layla placed her hand softly on the Thea's forehead and patted her.

Layla then whispered something to the Thea, and the Thea nodded and looked at the others.

Layla urged the others to follow and the others did so.

After following the Thea for a while, Axel whispered to Layla, "What did you say to the Thea?"

"I told her we were looking for Scarlett and that there might be a portal to a dimension where Scarlett was banished. The Thea knew that there was danger, so she agreed to help us and guide us to the tree.", replied Layla, whispering.

"How did you know how to calm the Thea?", questioned Axel.

"Thank the library of the Dummy Milennium Castle for that.", replied Layla, smiling.

"You know, we really do have to find a new name for the dummy castle.", stated Axel, chuckling.

Layla chuckled and looked around at the forest.

Meanwhile, Priscilla and Max were admiring the forest in awe.

"This forest is really beautiful. I wish we could stay here for a little longer…", stated Priscilla.

"We could always come back here.", said Max.

"True…", said Priscilla.

*"You know, I've been thinking. The text mentioned that Scarlett and Asher wanted to get hold of the element stones, **mainly**, the sun and moon element stones. How will they get hold of those element stones if no one knows where they went?", questioned Max.*

Priscilla thought for a while and said, "I guess that's another mystery for us to solve…"

"Yeah… Just like the one about Carla Books…", added Max.

Priscilla was about to ask something when Layla exclaimed, "The Thea found the portal!"

The four gathered around a tree that the Thea stood in front of. The Thea lifted her hoof and placed it on the tree bark.

A part of the tree bark dissolved and revealed a portal.

"This is the portal to the dimension where Scarlett and Asher are?", questioned Axel.

The Thea nodded slightly and walked aside.

The four glanced at each other and nodded. They then jumped into the portal together…

10 Ugaria

The four landed on the ground after falling a few feet down. They looked around in horror at the sight of the dimension they were in…

"I thought this dimension was only in stories…", uttered Max.

"You mean you know this dimension?", questioned Layla.

"This place is called Ugaria. It was said that the former holders of the sun and moon element stone, which means Scarlett and Asher were banished to this place…", replied Axel, looking around, terrified.

"Why are there dragons here as well?", asked Layla.

"They aren't supposed to be here. They're being controlled by those amulets…", replied Priscilla, pointing at the dragons' necks.

"Amulets? That sounds familiar!", exclaimed Max, recalling the witch.

"Wait a minute… I remember those dragons… They were in Volmania… Scarlett must've brought them here…", stated Axel.

"There are others as well… Look…", stated Layla, pointing at few dragons chained to the ground.
"Dragons, fairies and phoenixes… They must've caught them when they came out of this place…", said Priscilla, worriedly.

"There are soo many dark creatures guarding the creatures as well…", said Max.

Max gesticulated the others to hide behind a nearby rock with him.

"The dragons could spot us easily...", said Priscilla, watching the dragons shooting fire out of their mouths near the volcano.

"Well, the dark creatures are blind... We just need to do something about their hearing...", remarked Layla.

"Maybe I could stop the flow of our sound waves reaching their ears...", said Max, smiling.

"You can do that?", questioned Priscilla, holding onto one of her ears.

"Of course. The wind element stone makes it easier as well.", replied Max, confidently.

Axel took Nicole out of his backpack and said, "Hey, Nicole?"

Nicole, who was asleep in her globe, awoke. She smiled at the four, but when she saw Ugaria, her smile faded and her mouth fell open.

"Can you give us a glimpse of where Scarlett and

Asher are?", asked Axel.

Nicole gulped and said, "Luckily for you, I had been listening throughout the journey, so I know how Scarlett looks. It will be a piece of cake to find her!"

Soon, the globe glowed and showed Scarlett, who seemed to be on the other side of Ugaria.

"Asher, I am telling you these kids won't give up easily. They will find out about Ugaria and come here. I will have to use my last sun spell if we want our element stones back!", said Scarlett, trying to reason with Asher.

Asher turned around to protest. This was the first time the four had caught a glimpse of Asher. He had black hair and wore a cape.

"They may have the other element stones, but they can't keep us from getting our element stones back.", said Asher.

"They have 5 element stones, Asher. Our spell may work, but with them having 5 element stones, they could stop us…", stated Scarlett.

"They have minimized the number of our dark

creatures… But we still have atleast 30 of them…", said Asher.

"We also have the dragons. There are 5 of them. 3 of them copper dragons and 2 electrum dragons…", said Scarlett.

"The electrum dragons' love trading. Their love for trade has broken that control spell once, and you witnessed that in Volmania.", remarked Asher.

"We just have to perform the spell. We should get started, it will take 10 minutes at least.", stated Scarlett, turning to a mirror like structure.

Asher nodded and the two of them started chanting the spell.

The globe then showed Nicole again.

"We know that there are 30 dark creatures, and 5 dragons. The electrum dragons will be the easiest to break out of the spell. Once we have the electrum dragons by our side, they can help break the spell on the copper dragons.", stated Axel.

"The copper dragons can slow down any other creature with their breath. Ask me, I was a part of it. That was the worst experience of being slow…", added Max, recalling his slowing down due to the copper dragon's breath. "They also have powerful acidic breath. That could help with the weapons and dark creatures…"

"For the dark creatures, Max, you could use that spell to block their hearing…", stated Priscilla.

"I haven't used it in a while…", said Max, honestly.

"You can cast it on one of us now.", said Layla. "You could cast the spell on me."

"Are you sure? Losing your voice or your sense of hearing for even a short period of time is pretty terrible. I also lost my voice for a few seconds, which you very well why…", remarked Max, giving Layla a look, as he recalled what the keys of silence had done to his voice.

"Sorry about the keys of silence. And, I am sure I am ok with spell being casted on me.", said Layla, confidently.

Max nodded and closed his eyes for a while. His element stone glowed as he concentrated. When he opened his eyes, he asked, "Did it work?"

"*Did you cast the spell, Max?*", questioned Layla, clueless.

"*Yeah, I just did.*", replied Max.

"*Why aren't you saying anything??*", questioned Layla, frightened.

"*It worked!*", exclaimed Axel.

Although Axel was standing right next to Layla, Layla couldn't hear Axel either!

"*Can you remove the spell please, Max? The silence is literally killing the cat here.*", said Layla.

Max nodded and undid the spell with ease.

"*You should be able to hear us now…*", said Max.

"*I am able to hear you! By the way, you were right, Max! It's terrible to lose your sense of hearing…*", said Layla, holding onto one ear.

"*I told you!*", exclaimed Max.

"*Well, we know that the spell works. Now all we have to do is spilt up. I can help with the electrum dragons.*", stated Layla.

"I am taking care of the dark creatures. I might need help to fight them, just in case.", said Max.

"I'll go with you then.", added Priscilla.

"I'll help you with the electrum dragons, Layla. I brought a few valuable items from the castle before we left.", added Axel, holding the backpack up.

"Great! Sounds like a plan.", exclaimed Layla.

The four then spilt up. Axel and Layla headed towards the volcano, where the five dragons flew.

Max and Priscilla headed towards the dark creatures. Max effortlessly casted the spell on the dark creatures. After casting the spell, Max dropped a stone, to grab the dark creatures' attention.

However, none of them had a clue that a stone even dropped! The spell had worked!

Meanwhile, Layla and Axel made their way to the volcano. Axel placed a gem stone to grab the Electrum dragons' attention.

Not even a second had passed, that both the Electrum dragons spotted the gem stone.

Before either of them could grab the gem stone, Axel picked it up and he and Layla stepped in front of the dragons.

The dragons' amulets glowed, but they had no effect on the dragons. The dragons looked at the gem stone and smiled.

One of them said, "You knew our loving for trade would help us overcome the power of the spell…"

Layla smiled and nodded. She quickly took the amulets off the dragons to set them free.

Once she had done that, the second dragon introduced themselves, "I am Harry, and this is Elora, my sister."

"It's a pleasure to meet you. We need your help in setting the copper dragons free.", said Axel.

The dragons glanced at the gem stone again.

"After trading, of course. What would like to trade?", added Axel, smiling.

Axel took out a gem stone, similar to the previous one, only larger, brighter and red in color.

"The stone of the dragons… A gift given to a very few…", said Elora, smiling.

"I once received this, I was hoping you would help us, if we gave you this.", said Axel, ready to hand over the stone of the dragons.

Elora and Harry looked at each other and nodded.

"You have our help.", replied Harry, smiling.

Axel smiled back and handed the stone of the dragons to Harry's open palm. Harry hung it around his neck like a necklace.

Then, Elora asked, "How can we help you?"

"We want you to set the copper dragons free, then ask them to use their acidic breath and breath that slows others down on the dark creatures, there.", replied Layla, pointing to the dark creatures.

"Consider it done. But I must tell you this. Scarlett and Asher always have tricks ready up their sleeves. There is always more to the eye than what is seen…", stated Harry, wisely.

"That's almost the third time we heard that saying…", said Axel.

"Maybe you just need to hear it…", added Elora.

Harry and Elora then nodded and flew towards the copper dragons, leaving Layla and Axel near the volcano.

"Let's go! We now only need to stop Scarlett and Asher from casting that spell.", stated Layla, running over to the side where Max and Priscilla were.

Axel followed Layla and after a while, they reached the place where Max and Priscilla were.

"We need to get to Scarlett and Asher; the Electrum dragons have everything under control. They'll probably use their breath to leave the copper dragons confused and clueless.", stated Axel.

"Great! We've also been trying to set the other creatures here free, but the chains seem to be too strong, and the creatures are fast asleep. Asher must've casted a moon spell on them, assuming that he was a former holder of the moon element stone, since Scarlett was the former holder of the moon element stone…", remarked Max.

"They must be on the other side of Ugaria. I can

teleport us there.", said Layla.

The others nodded in agreement and Layla teleported themselves to a place father away from where they had previously been.

They looked around and spotted Scarlett and Asher, casting the spell on the mirror like structure.

Max used his element stone and send a gush of air, to cut off the chant that Asher and Scarlett narrated.

Asher and Scarlett realized this and turned to face the four.

"You were right, Scarlett. We should also have a backup.", said Asher, casting a spell to undo Max's spell.

Suddenly, five dark creatures appeared behind the four and four of the dark creatures caught hold of them.

Layla, Axel, Priscilla and Max struggled and used their all their strength to set themselves free, but in vain.

"You really thought I let only **four** dark creatures

absorb the aura from the crystal? In fact, they absorbed very little of it. These five dark creatures are the ones that absorbed the majority of the aura.", stated Scarlett, smiling.

"And only an Amethyst Pegasus can absorb that negative aura without being affected it…", stated Asher.

Scarlett and Asher continued their chanted, however had to start it over since they were interrupted…

~

A few minutes past, and Scarlett and Asher were still performing the spell…

The four, meanwhile, tried to use many spells to set themselves free from the grasp of the dark creatures, however, the dark creatures were too powerful.

Layla looked up at the sky, a twinkle of hope in her eyes. Suddenly, she spotted something in the cloudy sky.

She managed to grab Axel's attention and directed him to what she saw. Axel looked up and smiled.

Soon, the dark creatures started to groan, the green negative aura flowing out of them...

The green aura left the dark creatures completely, and the other aura which created them started to drain out of them as well!

After a few seconds, the dark creatures disappeared into thin air, as the aura flew upwards somewhere else.

The four turned her gaze upwards and spotted...
An Amethyst Pegasus!

The Mystery of the Element Stones

The four watched the Amethyst Pegasus fly through the air and land swiftly on the ground beside them.

The four then looked at each other and smiled.

They took off their element stones and held them out in front of them. The element stones turned to their original form and began to float in the air.

The four raised arms and gave their powers to the element stones. Once they had given their powers to the element stones, the element stones shot up in the sky, and there was a bright light.

Scarlett and Asher noticed this light and turned their gaze upwards, their spell completed.

The light faded and revealed the element stones floating in the air, accompanied by many other element stones! Soon, two other element stones appeared above them...

They were the sun and moon element stones! Scarlett and Asher thought that their spell had worked, and that they were the holders of the sun and moon element stones again! But they were half right...

The Mystery of the Element Stones

Their spell had worked, but like it is said, you can't force nature against her own will, it is also true that the element stones can't be forced to do something against their will.

All the element stones, water, fire, electricity, air, nature, animal, weather, ice, thunder and many others, combined and formed a new creature.

"Origina...", uttered Axel, weakly.

"Origina?", questioned the others.

"Origina is said to be the origin of all the element stones... The element stones are all a part of her...", replied Axel, looking at Origina.

The wolf-like creature looked at Scarlett and Asher in the eye and said, multiple voices overlapping, "You were the rightful owners of the element stones once, but there was something that made you change your goal... I shall give you a second chance to remember, but not a second chance of keeping the spells you learnt from the element stones with you..."

Origina then held up her paw and a light came out of it...

The Mystery of the Element Stones

It soon took away the remainder of the sun and moon magic from Scarlett and Asher, and also the spells connected to the element stones!

Scarlett and Asher then disappeared into thin air. Origina then turned to the four and stated, "You four have helped everyone… But I must tell you this, I have shifted Scarlett and Asher somewhere else, but even I can't separate all their sun and moon magic from them. I have drained all their other powers.

Remember, there is always more to the eye than what is seen… You must find out what happened to Scarlett and Asher that made them like this… Connect the dots and you shall find the answer to all your questions…"

Origina then glowed and separated into her element stones. The element stones scattered back to their respective homes, while the fire, electricity, water, air and nature element floated back to the four.

The fire element stone became a ring on Axel's fingers, the water and electricity element stones took the form of the necklace around Layla's neck, the air element stone became a necklace around Max's neck and the nature element stone became a bracelet around Priscilla wrist…

The element stones gave the four their powers back, and the four felt energetic again.

"Guys… Look!", exclaimed Max, pointing at the sky, where the sun shone brightly.

The ray hit the ground and soon, emerald green grass filled the land! The rays fell all over Ugaria and Ugaria retrieved her true form again!

The volcano turned into tall mountains, the lava turned into flowers and trees!

Stars from the sky shot down from the night sky, although the sun was still up!

They spotted Elora and Harry, flying with the other copper dragons, smiling, implying that there was no fear of the dark creatures.

The chained creatures were set free as the stars shot on their chains!

The Mystery of the Element Stones

The Amethyst Pegasus neighed and flew upwards into the sky, welcoming all the animals back to Ugaria.

"Wow! Ugaria changed a lot!", exclaimed Layla, looking around.

"Look the sun is coming up!", exclaimed Max, pointing towards the sky.

The night sky gave way to the light blue sky and the moon welcomed the sun as it exited.

All the mythical creatures once again entered their home with great joy!

The Amethyst Pegasus landed in front of the four and extended it's left wing, holding a letter out.

Layla took the letter and thanked the Pegasus. The Pegasus nodded and took flight, reuniting with its family.

"What does the letter say?", questioned Axel, curiously.

Layla opened the letter and read it. She then said, "It's from Origina… It says,

The Mystery of the Element Stones

'You have revived the beauty and glory of Ugaria.
I request you to solve another mystery related to
the ones you have been on. This mystery may help
you understand what happened to Scarlett and
Asher. Check the Dummy Millennium Castle, or
should I say, The Mysteria, for answers.

This mystery is about Rachel Winters and Noah
Winters… They were two famous explorers, who
traveled the various dimensions. However, they
disappeared without a trace.

You must track them down to know what
happened to Scarlett and Asher.

All the best, I hope you find the two explorers,
who were called, The Thunderbolts…'"

"The Thunderbolts? Sounds like a mystery we can
solve, right guys?", questioned Priscilla, smiling.

The other nodded in agreement and created a portal
back to the dummy Millennium Castle, or now
called, the Mysteria…

The four have solved the Mystery of the Element
Stones. Now, they have two mysteries that go
hand in hand. They now have to solve the Mystery
of the Thunderbolts, in order to solve the Mystery

The Mystery Series

Character Description

Main Characters:

Layla (19 years old) – Sky-blue eyes (from Amy), light red hair (from James)

Priscilla (19 years old) – Brown hair, Black eyes

Max (19 years old) – Brown hair, Brown eyes

Axel (19 years old, phoenix) – Half-black-half-purple hair, cyan eyes

Lord Asher – Black hair, amber eyes

Scarlett – Red Hair, brown eyes

Dark creatures – black in color, red eyes, sharp claws like those of a grizzly bear, speed like that of a panther.

Weaknesses of the dark creatures – don't possess magical abilities, however can dodge and reverse other spell, are blind and use their sense of touch and hearing to locate objects.

Strengths of the dark creatures - Ability to reverse spells, speed, strength, acute sense of hearing, absorb certain spells and gain greater strength!!

Other Main Characters:

Amy – Blonde hair, sky-blue eyes

James – Red hair, dark brown eyes

Marcelo - Black hair, Black eyes

Celia - Red hair, light Brown eyes

Katherine - Black hair, Brown eyes

Emma – blue eyes, gray hair

Emmy – blue eyes, gray hair

Phoebe – Half-blonde and Half-gray hair, black eyes.

Lucas – Half-black and Half-gray hair, sky-blue eyes

ABOUT THE AUTHOR

Shreya is 13 years old studying in class IX.

This is the young author's sixth book.

This book is Part V of her second book.

"The Mystery of the Waterfall of Life" (Part I) Published on amazon KDP select on Feb 2021.

"The Mystery of the Enchanted Forest" (Part II) Published on amazon KDP select on May 2021.

"The Mystery of the Old New Creatures" (Part III) Published on amazon KDP select on October 2021.

"The Mystery of the Questionable Past" (Part IV) Published on amazon KDP select on December 2021.

Another book written by this author:

"How to Confront Your Bullies and Haters"

All books by this author are available on amazon.com and Kindle (KDP Select).

Do stay tuned for more books that are in incubation.

Thank you □

www.ingramcontent.com/pod-product-compliance
Lightning Source LLC
Chambersburg PA
CBHW061243120726
48001CB00001B/111

Praises For...

The Making of an Orphan

"In her memoir titled *The Making of an Orphan,* Leslie Dean uses very personal stories to show the devastating impact intergenerational trauma can cause in a person's life. Being so vulnerable and sharing even the ugly stories is offset by her very strong desire to reach out to those who live in hopelessness and oppression. By telling how she came to understand her parents and how they formed her beliefs about who she was, we feel her pain in reliving those times. It also forces us to open our eyes and look at how we picture ourselves in the frame presented to us by our parents.

Who will benefit from reading her books? Anyone desiring to understand who they are and why they act the way they do and say the things they say! And when they recognize themselves in her stories and understand it doesn't have to stay the way it is, they can choose to reframe how they see themselves and to experience the healing so needed!"

—Lynette Wright, *Director of Outreach Ministries*

"My husband and I run a Christian retreat and conference center in Manns Choice, PA with a large outreach to military families. We offer church retreats here as well.

I met Leslie when she attended a retreat here. It was a joy to meet her and learn of the book she had written, *Forgiven Much.* After learning her story, we were honored to sell her book in our on-site bookstore. We have received positive feedback from guests who read it.

We are excited she has completed *The Making of an Orphan* because we have had guests talk to us about the need for help in dealing with, and working through, generational trauma. We also run an internship program and believe her story might help our interns work through their past issues.

The Lord has given Leslie great courage in sharing her story, and she does so in such a wonderful way that I find it hard to put her books down!"

—Dawn Robyn, *White Sulphur Springs Retreat and Conference Center*

"Most people today think of their upbringing as 'normal.' When trauma occurs, we have no concept of how many miles that is from our Heavenly Father's design for families. Instead of a Secure Base from which we are free to explore and then return, the distress is 'normalized.'

In *The Making of an Orphan*, Leslie Dean combs through the chapters of her life, seeing not only her trauma, but also the spawning ground of her parents' trauma. She helps us recognize that when we can see how our lives have been constructed, we can then find hope and healing through a personal connection with Jesus!

—Jeannette Hazel, *Biblical Counselor*